The
Glade

and other stories

The Glade

and other stories

by

Paul Bassett Davies

Contents

Seeing the Werewolf...1

Prussian Blue 17

I.F..29

Vulpine 37

Tommy the Voice 45

Warts...60

A Very Nice Man...80

Sweet Prince 83

Loss Adjustment..103

Prank versus Dick Move 115

The Glade 123

AUTHOR'S NOTE..158

Seeing the Werewolf

We both paid five euros to see the werewolf, and when we emerged from the narrow canvas passageway into a small space at the back of the tent it was just a normal guy sitting on a stool. He was wearing sandals, cargo shorts and a polo shirt, and reading a book.

This is bullshit, I said to Sarah.

The guy on the stool looked up and took off his reading glasses. Hello, he said, is there a problem?

I was about to tell him that yes, there appeared to be a problem concerning him not being a werewolf, when Sarah nudged me and directed my attention to the man standing behind me. He was positioned beside the entrance we'd just come through, which, I noticed, was also the only way out. He wore a blue suit that would have looked quite stylish if he'd been able to find one in his size, but I doubted they made them that large. He wasn't alone. A much smaller person was standing on the other side of the doorway but I couldn't tell if it was a man or a woman, or some combination of the two. You never know these days. Especially in Holland, even though we were in a bleak industrial area just north of Rotterdam. I looked hard at this second individual, whose gender remained elusive to me. It didn't help that the light in the tent seemed weirdly dense, or maybe it was the bottle of wine I'd shared with Sarah in the car. However, experience has taught me that when you're confronted by a pair of potential assailants, one of whom is an oversized lummox, always keep your eye on the smaller one because he – or she – is the one who's going to make a sudden move and stab you in the neck while you're worrying about how to deal with the big dude.

Sarah nudged me again. I turned to see that the guy who was meant to be a werewolf was now on his feet. He wasn't as big as the man beside the doorway but he was still on the large side.

He smiled. Perhaps you should look at me, he said in a pleasant voice that had almost no trace of an accent. After all, he continued, it's what you've paid for.

I told him he didn't look much like a werewolf to me.

Sarah giggled. Me either, she said.

I realised she was flirting with him.

He gave a throaty chuckle. Of course I don't look like a wolf now, he said, it's the middle of the afternoon!

Sarah laughed. She lurched unsteadily and clutched my arm. The bogus werewolf smiled at her with frank appreciation. She wagged a finger at him. I get it, she said, you only turn into a wolf at night, right?

The guy raised his eyebrows comically and nodded with earnest approval, as if a pair of dim schoolkids had finally got the point.

And what time, I said, does this place close?

He turned to me and frowned. Unfortunately, he said, local ordinances require that the funfair shuts down at dusk.

Sarah laughed again, long and hard, until she collapsed against me. She pointed a wavering finger at the guy. You bad, bad man, she gasped happily.

He spread his arms, then made a series of graceful, sweeping gestures up and down his body. But look at me, he said, see how hairy I am!

It was true that his legs were pretty hairy, and he seemed to have plenty of chest hair, growing up to his throat, visible at the open neck of the polo shirt. Which was an actual polo shirt, by the way, as in the brand, Polo by Ralph Lauren, and not a knockoff. I worked with knockoffs for a while, and I can spot them. He also had a thick, black beard that grew up to his cheekbones, and now he concluded his exhibition of himself by stroking the beard with both hands as if it were the luxuriant fur of a lovely but skittish animal.

Sarah reached out her arms. She wanted to join in the beard-stroking. She staggered forward, and I caught her around the waist and pulled her back as gently as I could. She didn't resist. Slowly I steered her backwards out of the entrance, taking care not to look at the people standing on either side of it.

The hairy man raised an arm in an exuberant salute. If you're leaving, he cried, farewell and go in peace, my friends!

I kept my arm around Sarah's waist as we walked away from the tent. She was pretty unsteady. I glanced back at the entrance, where we'd handed over our money to another man who was also on the large side. Part of his job, I suspected, was to discourage people like us who'd just emerged from the tent, having been ripped off, from informing people in the line that they, in turn, were about to be ripped off.

Right now the only people in the line were two stoned-looking teenage boys, and a young woman with a baby in a papoose arrangement on her chest and a little girl, no more than three, holding her hand. What the fuck was she thinking, taking little kids in there to see a werewolf?

None of it made sense, especially as the rest of the funfair was just a regular, travelling funfair, and everything was modern and tacky, with loud techno music and lots of flashing lights on the rides and the stalls.

Naturally, Sarah and I had gone to see the werewolf ironically, expecting the whole thing to be kitsch and unintentionally funny, and I guess we'd both imagined that some kind of effort would have been made – a cage, some fake fur and teeth, makeup, whatever – and the ineffectiveness of these efforts would have been part of the fun. But what had happened in there hadn't been fun.

We were a few yards beyond the funfair exit when Sarah suddenly sat down on the grass with her legs splayed.

I'm going to throw up, she said, and immediately an arc of vomit gushed from her mouth. She leaned forward. I tried to pull her hair out of the way but it wasn't really long enough to matter, so I settled for patting her on the shoulder. Her body heaved and she released another stream of spew. Some of it splashed back up from the ground and flecked her face.

We'd been drinking for several days, and that morning we'd taken some pills I'd bought in the club in Amsterdam, and we'd also done some lines of what may or may not have been coke. As I patted Sarah's back half-heartedly something told me we wouldn't be sleeping together again. Our whirlwind romance was drawing to a close, I felt.

But I was wrong, in a way. We decided to continue driving to Rotterdam, which was where we'd been heading when we saw the funfair and took a detour, and the journey was pleasant after I remembered I had some weed left. We arrived in the city as the sun was setting, and I asked Sarah if she wanted me to take her to the station. She shook her head. I got the feeling she was running low on money. Neither of us had anyone else to be with, and we didn't want to be alone.

We found a hotel not far from the city centre. It was a nondescript place, not too big, and I liked it for that reason and because I could still afford it. We crashed out for a couple of hours, then woke up at around midnight and made love. It was slow and sweet, maybe because we'd both decided it was over between us, and now we could just enjoy ourselves, no pressure. We went to sleep again afterwards and slept until noon.

We went out and bought some food and ate it in a park near the hotel. Even though we were only a mile from the city centre the area was solid and residential. It was restful to stroll around there, looking into the windows of unexciting shops. Both of us seemed in reasonably good shape after a binge that had begun when we hooked up in Amsterdam and lasted nearly a week. Now we were making a slow, soft

5

landing.

After another nap at the hotel we wandered back into the streets at around nine. We passed a couple of bars before we found one that seemed like the kind of place we wanted to be in. It was small, and although the crowd inside appeared relatively young the music wasn't loud enough to make much of an impression, which was a definite advantage.

But the big attraction was at the far end of the room, where almost the entire back wall was an aquarium tank. Behind a thick sheet of glass, eight feet high and twelve feet wide, a whole bunch of fish were mooching around.

There were four booths back there, with narrow tables at right angles to the glass, separated by low partitions. One of them was unoccupied and Sarah slid into it while I went to the bar.

It was only when we were drinking the beers I'd bought that we began to notice a couple of things about the fish. Firstly, there were a lot of them, and they often collided and tangled with each other. Secondly, several of them were very damn large. Even taking into account the magnifying properties of the thick plate glass, many were at least three feet long, and some were bigger. A couple of them were definitely some type of shark. But there were also plenty of regular fish, of the kind you'd find in a domestic fish tank. All things considered, there was an exceptionally wide range of aquatic life in there.

At first it was both unsettling and mesmerising to be sitting so close to all those fish, especially as some of the big predators had a habit of drifting past casually, then executing a sudden, swirling turn,

6

and zooming back to inspect you, shoving their snouts up against the glass. But we got used to it after a while.

I went to the bar again, and just as I was slipping back in opposite Sarah there was a huge commotion in the tank. The water churned and thrashed, then turned pink, and then red. Fragments of flesh and entrails drifted away in every direction, like shrapnel from a slow-motion explosion. One of the sharks circled around crazily, remnants of a smaller, less fortunate fish trailing from its jaws.

As all this happened several youngish men at the bar were giving a ragged cheer. They slapped each other on the back and exchanged fist-bumps. Some kind of bet had been settled and money changed hands over the bar. These guys, along with quite a few others in the room, were big, meaty types. Many of them wore camouflage pants and other garments with a military theme, but they didn't look fit enough to be soldiers, and a lot of them had prominent bellies. They seemed to be the kind of people who like to dress up in military gear, and go into the forest at weekends and fantasise about the end of civilisation.

My attention was caught by a man in the next booth, who'd been sitting with his back to us, and who now stood up. I'd been wondering about him for a while, mostly because he was wearing a small, go-pro style camera on his head. It was strapped down with canvass webbing over his thick, springy hair. He scanned the room, and as his gaze met mine we recognised each other. It was the werewolf.

We stared at each other in astonishment. After a moment he broke into a huge grin. Sarah turned to see who I was looking at and as their eyes met he gave her a shy, yearning glance followed by a debonair bow.

My friends, he said when he straightened up, I will join you, yes?

We told him he was welcome. He slipped out of his booth and into ours, sitting down next to Sarah.

Don't worry, he said, pointing to the camera on his head, I am an activist.

His name was Bruno, and what he told us in the next five minutes reminded me how very wrong I can often be about pretty much everything.

Firstly, the whole werewolf thing had nothing to do with the funfair. It was an experimental performance art project. He and his two colleagues had been given a grant by an arts foundation to perform the piece in a series of different contexts, and they'd paid the funfair to host them. The project's purpose was to challenge the expectations of an audience around the idea of monsters, and then to engage them in a shared narrative journey, creating an interactive contemporary myth based on the transformative celebration of the wolf that lurks within all of us. Unfortunately, Sarah and I left before we got to that part.

Next, Bruno revealed that when he and his friends weren't doing performance art, the three of them were in a circus. Bruno did a clown act, sword swallowing, and stage illusions. The big guy, Tancred, was a strongman who also performed what Bruno described as erotic drag ballerina dancing. Jana was an acrobat and contortionist.

I interrupted by asking if Jana was a woman.

Bruno laughed and said that yes, she was a woman. He gave me an odd look and told me Jana had been watching me on video. I asked him what he meant. He said there had been a camera in the tent. Hadn't we noticed?

No, I said, we hadn't.

He mentioned the release form we'd signed when we bought our tickets. I said I vaguely remembered signing something, but I'd thought it was all part of the flimflam, like an old-time publicity stunt, where they'd say you were being insured in case you had a coronary because the show was so scary. No, Bruno said, it was so they could film us. Jana had been reviewing the footage.

I said I'd been confused about her because I'd been unable to see properly in the tent. He explained that it had been full of dry ice, which probably contributed to my confusion, although he'd also noticed that Sarah and I were totally shitfaced. But it was probably the dry ice, he said magnanimously. The machine was very powerful, he said, and they used it a lot in their circus, which they performed in the same tent, and which seated only thirty people when employed for that purpose. He described the circus show as being very small scale, and magically intimate, so it was super effective at the end when the horse came on.

The horse?

Bruno told us they had a wonderful horse. A beautiful old animal, that emerged through a pair of curtains and paraded sedately around the tiny ring. It always sought out children in the audience, and would allow them to pat its nose. It seemed able to identify kids who were disabled in any way, and approached them, and nuzzled them, which invariably created wonder and delight. It was a lovely, enchanted animal, he said. They'd rescued it from a big, conventional circus, where it was being mistreated.

Bruno's face darkened. I hate cruelty to animals, he said, and that's why I'm here. They know me, all these macho bullshitters. I'm going to get this fucking place shut down, and they know it.

He gestured at the camera on his head and grimaced at the fish tank.

I'd noticed that Sarah had been gazing at Bruno intently, and whenever he looked at her something seemed to pass between them. At this point she shifted on the bench and said she needed to use the ladies' room. Bruno sprang up and ushered her out of the booth with great gallantry.

When he sat down again he leaned towards me. I'm sorry, he said in a low voice, but I have to tell you I am in love with your woman.

She's not my woman, I said.

His face lit up with a big smile. So, he said, it is okay if I attempt to make a romance with her?

I told him yes, it was okay to make a romance with her. I explained that I'd only known Sarah a week, and we were no longer an item, and I wished him well. He nodded gravely and shook my hand. It was nice of him to be so sincere about it but to tell the truth it didn't make much difference to me.

Sarah returned, and the smile she exchanged with Bruno as she squeezed past him, taking her time, made me think she had a pretty good idea what was going on.

Just after Sarah sat down, a muscular middle-aged man with very short hair came out from behind the bar carrying a big pail. He went to the booth at the far end of the aquarium tank, and spoke curtly to the couple in there. They stood up quickly and shuffled aside. He hopped up onto the bench and opened a hatch on top of the tank. Raising the pail, he tipped a cascade of slithering new arrivals into the water. They splashed and squirmed around too much to tell exactly what they were, but none of them looked particularly large. Maybe they were piranhas.

As the short-haired man – who seemed to be the proprietor – stepped down from the bench he caught sight of Bruno. He strode over, swinging the pail, and stood glaring down at Bruno, who stared at him impassively. The proprietor said something in Dutch. He sounded angry.

Bruno nodded at me and Sarah and said, in English, that we were English.

I'm American, Sarah said.

Fuck you, the proprietor said, in English, and then continued speaking to Bruno in Dutch, pointing at the camera on his head. He finished and waited for a reply. Bruno said nothing. The proprietor turned and strode away.

Bruno smiled grimly at us. This is not Amsterdam, he said. It's not a place in a fairy tale. This can be a hard city.

He took out his phone and started texting as he continued speaking to us, telling us that the guy wanted him to hand over his camera and get out.

Shouldn't we go, I asked.

Bruno shook his head. It's all right, he said. Nothing bad will happen.

I looked over Bruno's shoulder and saw that the proprietor was back behind the bar, watching us angrily. Bruno followed my gaze and turned to look at the guy, who narrowed his eyes and pointed to Bruno's camera, and then at his own his watch. Bruno shook his head. He turned back to me. Don't worry, he said.

The proprietor began whispering to three of the camouflage asshole types propping up the bar. They all turned and gave us hard, tough-guy stares, then went back into a huddle.

I didn't like the way this was going, and I thought maybe I should try to persuade Bruno that we should leave before things escalated any more.

Too late. The three wannabe soldiers pushed themselves off their bar stools and fell in behind the proprietor as he walked towards us again.

Before they reached us Bruno glanced at the door and waved. Two figures entered the bar and strode the length of the room to our booth, arriving at the same time as the proprietor and his goons. The newcomers were Bruno's colleagues, Tancred and Jana. Now that I could see Tancred clearly, without the hindrance of dry ice and alcohol, he looked quite amiable. But there was no denying his massive physical bulk, and he was still bursting out of his suit, which was a green one today.

And Jana still looked very small beside him, not least because she was, in fact, no more than five feet tall at the most. She was extraordinary. I couldn't take my eyes off her, and when she looked at me I felt a jolt of excitement. She had huge, expressive eyes beneath a crop of spiky red hair, and a very wide mouth with full lips. She put her hands on her hips and grinned at me, revealing prominent teeth. I loved the way she stood. She was wearing tight leopard-print leggings and a sleeveless denim jacket over a sports bra. Her short, squat body looked strong and compact.

As I took all this in, a tense standoff was developing. The proprietor and his friends were flicking their eyes between Bruno and Tancred, making calculations. They'd clearly dismissed me and Sarah from the equation, probably correctly, and they weren't paying much attention to Jana, either. Not, that is, until she stepped forward, glanced at each of the men in turn with a confident smile, and then, with a deft movement, flipped her jacket open to display a small gun taped inside it. Something about the dullness of the metal and the worn grip made me think the gun was real. No one else seemed to doubt its authenticity, either. Everyone became very still.

Jana let the jacket fall back into place. Bruno placed his hands on the table and looked at me and Sarah. Let's go, he said.

We stood up. The proprietor and his cohort made no attempt to stop us as we walked out.

When we got outside Bruno already had his arm around Sarah's waist. She told me she'd call me tomorrow about her stuff at the hotel. Tancred said he was in a rush to see his boyfriend. He smiled, performed a pirouette, and walked away.

I muttered something about the hire car at the hotel.

You can leave it, Jana said, and if you come to my place, I will ride you.

Bruno snorted and squeezed her shoulder. What she means, he said to me, is that she will give you a ride there. On her bicycle.

Jana poked him in the ribs. I know what I mean, she said.

They laughed, and Sarah joined in. I felt like a teenager.

Bruno and Sarah sauntered away, lurching into each other. Jana's bike was leaning against the wall beside the entrance to the bar. She pulled it upright and pointed to the saddle.

You can sit, she said, and I will pedal.

Jana straddled the bike, holding it steady for me. It was a big old-fashioned, sit-up-and-beg ladies' model with no crossbar. As I started to sit on the seat she stopped me. It's easier sideways, she said.

I balanced myself side-saddle.

Hold me, Jana said, and scooted the bike forward.

I held her hips as she stood on the pedals, cycling powerfully over the cobbles. It was like I was a prince, or maybe a prize.

Jana left her bike in the hallway of an old, narrow house, and led me up three flights of stairs. Her flat was just a room with a bathroom and kitchenette. A bed took up most of the space. Jana closed the door and threw off her jacket. She kicked off her shoes, rolled down her leggings, and stepped out of them.

She stood there in her underwear and held out her hands. I took them in mine and she began to pull me towards her gently. As we reached kissing range I resisted for a moment, just to see what would happen.

What happened was that Jana did some kind of very fast Judo flip on me, and I landed on the bed, looking up at her and gasping. She sprang onto the bed and straddled me, gripping my wrists and forcing my arms apart until I was spread-eagled beneath her. She was like a beautiful ape. She licked her lips in a pantomime of lasciviousness, then flashed me that huge grin.

So, she said, do you want to join the circus?

I was very aroused, and now I felt an unfamiliar rush of weird exhilaration. Maybe it was happiness. I had no idea what was coming next.

As Jana slowly leaned forward, pressing her body down onto mine, a flash of silvery light caught the corner of my eye. I turned my head to see that over Jana's shoulder, outside her window, the moon was almost full.

Yes, I said, I want to join the circus.

Jana seemed to be getting closer to me all the time. Her huge, unblinking eyes gazed into mine. They were pale grey with tiny flecks of yellow. I tried to raise myself up so I could kiss her but I couldn't. She had me pinned down and she was extremely strong.

She lowered her head. Are you sure, she whispered in my ear.

Yes, I said. Her bare arm and shoulder were next to my face, and the moonlight from behind her silhouetted the fine hair that covered them.

I felt her tongue licking my ear. Its surface was rough and it was drenched in saliva. You will need a safe word, she said.

I felt a powerful wave of energy rippling through all my muscles. I tried to flex my arms but I still couldn't move them beneath her grasp. Even though I felt exceptionally strong, she was stronger.

Werewolf, I said.

Werewolf?

Yes, I said, that's my safe word. Werewolf.

I felt her body convulse against mine as something erupted deep inside her and surged up to her throat. She threw back her head and laughed.

I laughed too. We allowed the laughter to overwhelm us, thrashing and bucking against each other as we clung on for dear life.

Slowly my hysteria drained away. But Jana didn't stop.

She went on and on. She was howling with laughter.

Then she was just howling.

Prussian Blue

Kelly's problem was that her dad tasted too gritty.

She wanted to make a cheese sauce, maybe using Parmesan and Gruyere. That could work. Plus it needed to be a little spicy. She was improvising, but the starting point had to be a béchamel, as a base, which meant that her dad needed to be ground down to a fine powder, as fine as flour, and it wasn't happening. She'd already made two attempts at the roux, and when she tested them they were like the paste the bitchy dental hygienist used for scraping her teeth. Yikes.

She changed the blades in the food processor again, and tipped another small portion out of the urn. She turned the dial to its highest setting, held down the lid of the glass jug and pressed the button. The machine whined and a churning grey cloud appeared behind the glass. Looking good. She kept the button pressed for at least a minute. But when she let go and the blades whirred to a stop she could see it hadn't worked. The little nubbins of bone were too stubborn. And the jug was too large. The portions she was using just rattled around in there without getting milled properly. But she couldn't risk filling up the jug unless she was sure it would work, and she wasn't. There was a limit to how much of her dad she could afford to waste in a failed experiment.

Then she remembered the coffee grinder. Unbelievable. Why hadn't she thought of that first? Duh.

She fetched the grinder from the other end of the kitchen and paused to listen at the door on her way back. Not that she needed to.

Mum was at work today, and so was uncle Mike. The only other person in the house was Shireen, who was meant to be looking after her in the daytime during the school holidays. Yeah, right. Kelly knew her sister wouldn't come down from her bedroom no matter how much noise Kelly made in the kitchen. For one thing, everyone was used to her being in there, doing her cookery.

'Our little trainee chef!' her mother always said. 'Only nine, and she's already a better cook than me!'

Sometimes uncle Mike would say something like, 'Yeah, well that's not too difficult, is it?' and that was a bad sign. But if he grinned, and said Kelly was a smart kid, and when was Mum going to put her to work, to keep them all in a style he could definitely become accustomed to, then things were probably going to be okay for a while.

For another thing, Shireen didn't give a shit what Kelly did, as long as it didn't cause her any problems. Kelly could go where she wanted, and watch whatever she wanted on TV or online, as long as Shireen could stay upstairs and message her friends, and send her boyfriend photos of herself in her underwear, or maybe in nothing at all, depending on how "horny" she was feeling. Since she'd turned fourteen, just after Christmas, she'd started using that word a lot.

But Kelly knew that even if something bad happened, like maybe she broke something in the kitchen, Shireen wouldn't be in trouble. Mum was a bit scared of her now, that was the truth. And uncle Mike couldn't do anything, not since the night when Kelly heard him lurching into Shireen's room, and then a big commotion, and then he wasn't around for a couple of weeks. That was two months ago, and since he came back he'd had to keep his temper under control, especially around Shireen.

The only time Kelly had needed to be careful in this whole process was when she retrieved the urn from the hole in the garden. The spot under the tree was visible from Shireen's bedroom, and if she saw Kelly digging up their dad's ashes that would have been too much to ignore, even for her. Kelly waited until Shireen wanted to go out for the whole day, and promised not to rat on her.

When she started digging she found out it was pretty hard work, and it took a long time. She'd only just managed to get the hole filled in again and the turf laid back on top before her sister got home, just ahead of Mum.

It was their mother who insisted on Dad's urn being buried in the garden. Uncle Mike had tried to persuade her that the ashes should be scattered, somewhere on the coast, where they used to fish together.

They started arguing right after the funeral, when everyone had finished the sandwiches and drinks and gone away.

'It's what he would have wanted,' Mike said.

'Why?' Mum said. 'Why would he want to be blown around all over the place in the cold and the wet? Anyway, he only went fishing a few times, and he didn't even like it that much!'

Mike got up in her face. 'You have no idea.'

'Yes I have! I was married to him for ten years before you even met him! I know what he did and didn't like!'

Mike frowned angrily and glanced at Kelly and Shireen. They knew he wasn't really their uncle, of course, but he wanted everyone to act like he'd always been part of the family.

Mum continued regardless. 'I'll tell you what he liked,' she said, 'he liked sitting under that tree with a cup of tea and reading his book!'

The veins on Mike's neck bulged. 'You have no fucking idea!'

'Don't speak to me like that! Not after what I've been through!'

'What we've been through, you mean! I'm part of this!'

'Stop it! I can't take it! I'm in bits here!' Mum burst into tears and tried to gather her daughters into her arms but Shireen squirmed away and ran upstairs. Kelly allowed herself to be hugged.

But it was strange, she couldn't really remember seeing her father sitting in the garden very much. Maybe he'd liked doing it before he got ill, although Kelly couldn't remember much about that, either.

'Oh yes,' Mum said when Kelly asked her about it at bedtime, 'he'd been very poorly. But he was so brave and he didn't want to upset you kids, so he kept it from you. He loved you so much!' She started crying again, and Kelly put her arms around her neck and let her mother sob into her hair.

When uncle Mike had dug the hole under the tree Kelly stood in the garden watching him. Eventually Mike straightened up and looked at her for a while, breathing heavily. Then he started explaining about foxes and dogs, but Kelly turned away and went back into the house because she didn't want to think about her father being eaten.

And yet here she was, trying to cook him into a meal. She giggled to herself, and then felt bad about it. And then she didn't. Dad would have laughed, she was sure. He was always laughing.

She'd got the idea when she was watching National Geographic channel. She loved seeing all the animals and the different countries with mountains and rivers and forests and huge, empty spaces. They looked like places where anything could happen, and she thought about them before she went to sleep and had adventures there.

But you also saw some pretty amazing people in those shows too, especially the remote tribes. Some of them were cannibals, although the presenter said they didn't do it any more. But Kelly got the feeling they still did it. Especially when the chief talked about the ceremonies and rituals they used to perform. Kelly watched the brightly coloured feathers in his headdress bobbing up and down as he nodded and smiled, and she knew what that smile meant, even if the presenter didn't. Give me a break, she thought, that guy and his friends are still snacking on human flesh. There was a definite twinkle in his eye.

But the really interesting part was when he said they ate people to get their powers. Like, if they killed a great warrior, they ate him so they could get his warrior strength. The chief added that if they wanted to get someone's wisdom they ate his brain, and if they wanted "many children" they ate his "loins," which Kelly thought was pretty funny. But it got her thinking.

It was only a few days since she'd realised uncle Mike was going to be her new dad. She could see that Mum and Mike had already decided. She didn't have a vote. But what if she could change uncle Mike, and turn him into someone who was more like her dad? Was that even possible? The cannibals certainly thought so, and they seemed pretty cool to Kelly.

She didn't have much choice about which part of Dad she wanted uncle Mike to eat. She looked at the stuff in the urn, which was like a mixture of ash and sand and gravel. Who knew which parts were his heart, or the bit of his brain that made him funny? She understood she'd have to feed all of her dad to uncle Mike.

*

The coffee grinder did an outstanding job. Kelly ended up with a powder she could mix with flour and use for the roux. She tested a batch and although it still had a taste of ash, she was sure she could disguise it in some type of cheesy, spicy potato dish. Mike would eat anything with potatoes in it, especially if she crispy-fried them before baking them in the sauce. And she'd use plenty of curry powder and cumin, too. A weakness for spicy food was about the only thing uncle Mike ever really had in common with her father, Kelly thought. Dad's favourite treat was going to an Indian restaurant, and Shireen also liked that type of meal. Dad would do a silly, slouching walk and tease her about the way she and her friends talked, and Kelly would explode with laughter because he totally nailed the fake accent they all put on, and even though Shireen rolled her eyes she couldn't stop herself from smiling.

But as Kelly planned out the recipe she knew she had another problem. How could she fix things so that nobody except uncle Mike would eat what she was going to make?

Sometimes Kelly believed in God, sometimes she didn't. On the day she realised uncle Mike's birthday was coming up she was like, Hallelujah, praise the Lord.

She could say she'd made the food as a present for him. Tell him she didn't have any money to buy a gift but she really wanted to give him something. Perfect. And it would make him think she'd got used to the idea of him being her new dad, and was okay with it. Which she was, if it all worked, and he became more like her old dad. The real one.

*

She sat at the kitchen table watching uncle Mike eat.

Her mother had beamed when Kelly presented the food to him. Mike seemed pretty pleased too, especially as she'd made him pork chops to go with the potatoes. Everyone else was having fish pie.

After a few mouthfuls of food Shireen started using her phone. Mum put down her knife and fork.

'Can't you leave that bloody thing alone for one minute?'

'It's important,' Shireen muttered, 'Alison's been dumped and she's, like, totally going to kill herself.'

'No she's not. And remember the rule? Plus it's Mike's birthday, so please put it down.'

'All right, all right,' Shireen said, but she didn't stop.

'Do as your mother says,' Mike said, using his quiet voice. Bad sign.

Shireen glanced up at him and carried on.

'Shireen,' Mike said.

She didn't look up. 'What?'

'Your mother told you to put it down.'

Shireen sighed. She placed the phone carefully beside her plate and folded her arms.

'Thank you,' Mike said. 'Now perhaps we can—' He broke off and frowned. He ran his tongue over his teeth then gave a little cough as if he wanted to clear his throat.

'You all right, love?' Mum said.

'Fine. It's nothing.' Mike glanced at Kelly. He gave her a quick smile. 'Very tasty. Nice work, Kel. Good girl.' He took another bite of his food and chewed it slowly. He stopped chewing. He reached into his mouth and removed something. He held it up and looked at it, moving his tongue around the inside of his mouth.

Kelly couldn't look away.

'What is it?' Mum said.

'Bit of bone, I think,' Mike said.

'Must be from the chops.'

Mike looked down at his plate. 'No, it was in the spuds. In with the sauce.' He raised his eyes and squinted closely at the gobbet of food he was holding. His mouth hung open and Kelly could see the fillings in his teeth.

'What's wrong?' Mum said. She stared at Mike. He was breathing loudly. Finally he turned his gaze on Kelly.

She didn't move a muscle.

Mike's face seemed to ripple. 'What's in this food?' he hissed at Kelly.

She couldn't breathe.

Shireen looked up from her phone. 'What the fuck?'

Kelly couldn't tear her eyes away from Mike's face.

'Kelly,' her mother said, 'what have you done?'

Mike jumped up, knocking his chair over. He flung open the door that led into the back garden and ran out.

Shireen and Mum stared at the open door. Kelly waited.

Mike reappeared in the doorway. His face was grey. 'You fucking dug him up you little bitch!'

Mum was on her feet now, standing in front of him. 'What are you talking about? What's she done?'

Mike shoved her aside. 'You did, didn't you?' he shouted at Kelly.

Kelly tried to speak but her mouth was dry.

Mike made a howling sound and bit his fist.

Mum backed away from him.

He looked wildly around the kitchen then dropped to his knees and tore open the doors to the space under the sink with such force that one of the hinges broke. He started throwing things out behind him like a frantic animal digging a burrow, scrabbling and grunting.

Mum edged towards him and reached out to touch his back. 'What is it, Mike? Tell me.'

'Die!' Mike yelled with his head still in the cupboard, 'die!'

Mum recoiled. 'What?!'

Mike shuffled backwards until he could stand up. 'For clothes! Colouring! Blue colouring! Anything!'

Kelly realised he'd been saying dye, not die.

'Clothes dye,' Mike shouted, his voice hoarse, 'blue dye, anything blue!' His whole body was trembling. 'Ink! What about blue ink?'

Mum shook her head. 'We haven't got ink. Except in the printer…'

'No! It's got to be blue!'

'Why? What's happening?'

'Fucking thallium!' Mike shouted and ran to the utility cupboard. He threw open the door and pulled out a can of paint. He tore at the lid with his fingers.

'What's thallium?' Mum said.

Mike's eyes were hollow. 'In the rat poison!' he hissed, still clawing at the lid of the paint tin. His fingernails were bleeding. 'I couldn't risk buying it, could I? It was old shit, years old, from my mate's dad's shed. And they used to put thallium in it back in those days, understand? Oh Jesus Christ!'

Mike slammed the tin of paint down on the table. He glanced at Shireen. She was staring at him, trying not to let him see she was holding her phone again, texting by touch.

'What the fuck are you doing?' Mike shouted. He reached across the table and tore the phone from her hands. He hurled it against the wall and it smashed. Shireen shrank back into her chair. Mum started sobbing.

Mike picked up a knife from the table. Shireen screamed. Mike began using the knife to prise the lid off the can of paint.

'For… fuck's… sake,' Mum said, taking in big gulps of air as she sobbed, 'he was cremated! It was all burned!'

'It's radioactive!' Mike said. 'Not radioactive, but it's the fucking same. Thallium stays in the body!' The lid flew off the can, spraying blue paint everywhere. Mike turned to the sink and raised the can.

'What are you doing?' Mum said in a croaking voice.

'Prussian Blue. Antidote.' Mike took a deep breath, opened his mouth and tipped the can up. A big dollop of paint dropped into his mouth. He spluttered, then doubled over and retched, his whole body heaving. He raised his head. His mouth and chin were dripping with bright blue paint.

Shireen ran from the room. Mike dropped the can on the floor and staggered after her. 'Don't you fucking dare!' he yelled, his voice making a horrible bubbling sound.

Kelly heard the front door being opened and Mike yelling 'Fuck!'

Mum sank to the floor with her back against the fridge. Mike reappeared in the doorway. 'Catch her,' he wheezed. Kelly and her mother didn't move. Mike shook his head. Flecks of paint flew in an arc around the kitchen. 'Hospital,' he gasped. 'I gotta go. Don't fucking say anything to them.' He stumbled out.

Mum buried her head in her hands. 'I'm sorry,' she moaned, 'I'm so sorry.'

Kelly went upstairs. She didn't know exactly what would happen next, but she knew the police would come.

She turned her computer on, and opened the bottom drawer of her desk to make sure the tin of Prussian Blue dye was still there. She'd been careful to spit out the tiny samples she tasted when she was experimenting with the sauce, but it was best to be safe. And now she needed to erase her browser history. Ever since she'd figured out how they killed Dad she'd done a lot of research. Of course, the police could still find things, on the hard drive, but why would they look? She was just a little girl who missed her daddy and was trying to get him back. She'd even made careful diary entries about seeing the cannibals, and getting the idea.

She glanced at herself in the mirror and practised her wide-eyed look. For fuck's sake, she thought, I'm only nine.

I.F.

It happens to all of us in our profession, so I'm told. There's always a moment of shock, because you never remember the last time, to begin with.

Let's say you're in a garden, and it's a sunny afternoon. There's a kid there, a boy with a few freckles on the bridge of his nose, and he wants you to play some complicated game with him, about robots that change into other things and fight monsters or ghosts or aliens or other robots or whatever. Just when you're getting into it, his mother calls him into the house. Naturally, you go inside with him. And the mother asks the kid what he's been doing, has he been playing, and he shrugs and mumbles, and she gets all cute and asks, Hey, have you been playing with Asquith, how is Asquith anyway? Then she turns to this other young mother type who's having coffee with her and she says, as if it's the most adorable thing in the world, Isn't it funny, I don't know where he got it from, but what a strange name, don't you think, to give his imaginary friend?

Then it all comes back to you.

It's not always a kid. You'd be surprised. Maybe a guy in a suit is ranting about how he lost his job, and you're thinking, Wow, how long do I have to listen to this? Then a woman shows up and says, Hi Carl, I just heard, and not only does she ignore you but suddenly the guy who was venting forgets about you too, and you're like, Oh, I remember, I'm not here.

And sometimes the adult isn't even a new client. You got the job when they were five years old, and now they're forty-eight and they still want you around, so they haven't terminated you.

But the client I'm going to tell you about was a kid. Six years of age. Name of Alfie. And I'm Stoffard. No, I have no idea. Sometimes they make the names up, or sometimes it's something they've overheard, or misheard. One time I was Mercy, because the kid had been to France. It's not always a freaky name, sometimes we're something blah like Dave or Chantelle, but much of the time, when it comes to naming an IF (as we refer to ourselves), kids use their imagination.

Alfie was a genuinely nice individual, and he didn't have many reasons to be. He took a lot of crap from the other kids at school, and some of the teachers too. His mother did the best that someone who wakes up crying and has vodka for breakfast can do, and his father wasn't around much, and when he was around he made life even worse for everyone because he was a total dick. Strangely enough he had an IF, too. The first time I saw the dad, I noticed an elderly dude beside him who looked like he'd prefer to be somewhere else. We're not allowed to communicate, and if we try we're in big trouble (which is what this story is about), but whenever the father showed up I gave the IF a sympathetic little nod. He seemed pretty cheerful under the circumstances. I think he knew his contract didn't have long to run, because what the mother drank by the glass the father took by the bottle, in addition to being a world-class drug abuser. Sure enough, he

OD'd when I'd been with Alfie about three months, and damn if the boy wasn't heartbroken. But a dad is a dad, even if he's a turd.

Alfie was more messed up than ever after that, but he never lost his sweet nature. He continued to invent illnesses for me, so he could be extra kind to me. I was frequently afflicted with a rare but curable virus, and I was very accident prone. I often had sprains, fractures, bruises and minor cuts, and Alfie took great care of me.

You didn't have to be a shrink to see the kid wanted someone to love.

The new family that moved in next door seemed pretty normal. Two parents, two kids, one granny, one dog; no alcoholics, no junkies, no shy, awkward uncles who turn out to be killing hitchhikers with a chainsaw.

But there's no such thing as a normal family, believe me. So, while the prospect of happiness looked better on their side of the fence than on Alfie's, the roses in that garden had thorns as sharp as any others. But the thorns came later.

What came first was Hannah. She was the same age as Alfie and she was a knockout. The first time Alfie saw her she was standing in front of her new house and identifying her bedroom window for the benefit of a big old stuffed giraffe that she'd just dragged out of the removal van. Maybe the giraffe wasn't paying attention, because Hannah poked him in the neck and spoke very sternly to him, but then she broke into a giant, goofy smile, and gave him a big hug. I noticed that Alfie was holding his breath, then he let it out with a quiet little gasp when Hannah administered the hug. He didn't stand a chance.

And neither did I, because the other thing I noticed was Jazzinka. I only found out she was called Jazzinka later, when Hannah told Alfie about her IF, and Alfie told Hannah about me, when they were camping in the African jungle, under an old blanket slung across the clothes line in her back garden and pegged into the grass with kebab skewers. That was a lovely afternoon. The sun was shining through the blanket, and it was hot inside that little tent. Jazzinka and I were huddled in there too, of course. We smiled at each other as we inhaled the smell of fungus and mothballs from the blanket, mingled with the warm aroma of two sweaty, grubby little six-year-old bodies: the scent of innocence with the faintest tang of pee. We smiled, and we shouldn't even have acknowledged each other's existence.

Two days later it was raining, and we were guests at an elaborate tea party that Alfie and Hannah laid on in her garden shed. Three red plastic plates and a small blue cup circulated at breakneck speed, offering an array of jellies, cakes, biscuits, sweets, sandwiches, tea, lemonade, beer, wine, crocodile wee-wee (hysteria was kicking in), whisky, coffee, vodka, and finally a pudding they referred to as proffytroles, whose composition was a matter of conjecture between them, as neither of them had tasted it in real life, although they both agreed it was mostly chocolate, and certainly delicious, and went into ecstasies of pleasure as they gorged on huge, invisible mounds of it.

By the end of the party Jazzinka and I had abandoned any effort to ignore each other. She was tall and dark and slender with cool grey eyes that were also blue or brown. Her skin rippled and changed colour and she moved like a mythical bird or a snake or a lanky schoolgirl. I was less well defined. Where she was changeable, I was more like a work in progress. But Jazzinka seemed to like me anyway.

We hooked up again at the weekend during a visit to the zoo – located in Hannah's bedroom – which the two children populated with a variety of exotic creatures unknown to modern biology, in addition to the usual animals. They got very engrossed in feeding the fantastical creatures, and deciding how dangerous they were, leaving me and Jazzinka plenty of time together. I could see she was very fond of Hannah, and perhaps she sensed how much I liked Alfie, and maybe our tenderness for our charges – I can't bring myself to call those kids clients – kind of spread out, and flowed between us, and informed our feelings for each other. The room was full of happiness, and a wild energy.

The next day I had a terrible thought. Hannah and Alfie were becoming close friends. I was pretty sure Alfie would still want me around for a while, even if he wasn't lonely any more, but what if Hannah decided she no longer needed her IF? I had a vision of Jazzinka fading away before my eyes, and it gave me a sick, unsteady feeling. I started to think about the future, which I'd never done before. What if I lost her?

But a week later we were both still there, as spectators to a Ping-Pong game in Hannah's basement. We stood close, much closer than we should have done, and it felt like we were drinking each other in, or absorbing one another. We didn't have to say anything to understand we were in love.

We both knew we were heading for disaster. What we were doing simply wasn't permitted. The laws of nature, logic, and possibility are pretty flexible, to tell you the truth, but our code of ethics isn't. At the very least we risked an Intervention. We would be terminated without prejudice to the client, who would wake up one day with no memory of having an IF. Meanwhile the offending IF would have a long time to think it over, in a very lonely place, before even being considered for another contract.

I think Alfie and Hannah sensed what was happening with me and Jazzinka, or maybe they were making it happen. I can't really get into the existential issues here, but if you want a rough idea of how it works, think of it as a collaboration: yes, people invent their imaginary friends, but I also have a life of my own.

And so did Jazzinka, and we were getting desperate. What could we do? We considered telling Hannah and Alfie we wanted to quit, asking their blessing, and running away to... where? We didn't know what would happen if we tried to exist independently of a client. Maybe we'd die. I don't mean die like being terminated, which is more like ending a job, going to sleep, then starting a new job. I mean die.

But we made up our minds to risk it. We had to be together, and we couldn't wait for Alfie and Hannah to come up with the idea, although they'd get around to it sooner or later. Hannah would say, Hey, why don't Stoffard and Jazzinka get married? And Alfie would love it. He'd chuckle, and start digging a hole to bury wedding presents.

But whatever they imagined marriage to entail, I was pretty sure it wouldn't include the kind of conjugal intimacy Jazzinka and I had in mind. And how could we tell them? They were six years old. There was only one thing for it: we had to run. But before we even got started, events overtook us.

It was all because of the dog. She was a yappy little thing about the size of a squirrel, and Hannah's mother only bought her to annoy her husband. He retaliated by pretending to adore the animal so he could pay it more attention than he paid his wife. It was that kind of marriage. They used Hannah and her baby brother like bargaining chips, and the only thing they had in common was selfishness. The mother was a controlling bitch, and the father was a womanizing pig. That was why Granny was around: to help her daughter keep an eye on him. But lust is like a toxic cloud, and it doesn't discriminate. Hannah's mother may have thought her husband wouldn't see anything to attract him in the lonely, alcoholic single mother next door, but what a man like that sees is simply the opportunity.

He started screwing her within weeks of them moving in. He'd take the dog for a walk, ambling along the street until he knew Granny could no longer see him from her bedroom window, then he'd snatch the dog up, phone Alfie's mother, race around the block, and come in through the side door of the house. They did it when Alfie was at school, or when he was in bed, or even when he was playing in Hannah's garden.

One evening Alfie's mother got the call, so she opened the side door as usual and began to undress. When he arrived, he was in such a hurry he didn't close the door properly. The dog wandered out, chased a pigeon across the road and got hit by a car. Granny heard the commotion, hobbled out, and saw the dog under the front wheel of a Toyota. She followed her instinct all the way to Alfie's mother's bedroom, to be confronted by her son-in-law's blotchy, pumping buttocks.

The family moved out two weeks later. They took Hannah away, and Jazzinka went with her. I thought Alfie's heart would break.

Mine too.

*

I can't leave Alfie now. For the last few weeks he's been watching a TV series about the history of medicine, and so far I've had bubonic plague, malaria, tuberculosis, hepatitis and Ebola, and now I'm coming down with what could either be dengue fever or Munchausen's Syndrome by Proxy, depending on the diagnosis. Alfie's looking after me very well, and I'll get over it. But I won't get over Jazzinka.

Maybe I'll find her again. It won't be any time soon, because it looks like Alfie's mother is heading for an early grave, and he'll need me more than ever. But he'll endure, I think, and one day he'll let me go. Then there will be another job and another client, and then another. And maybe, one day, I'll be playing in another sunny garden with another little boy, and we'll notice a little girl who's just moved in next door peeping over the fence, and I'll sense a presence, and then I'll see her.

And if not? Well, so be it. I'm no stranger to loneliness, and there's no reason an imaginary friend can't have an imaginary friend of their own.

Vulpine

At 6.50 on a Tuesday evening a young woman arrives home from her job in the City, where she works as a maritime lawyer for a large, well-respected firm. She enters her penthouse apartment and takes off her high-heeled shoes as she walks to the master bedroom. She stops in the doorway. On the carpet at the foot of her bed is a dead fox.

There is no indication as to how it could have got there. The windows are secure, and everything in the apartment appears to be exactly as the woman left it in the morning. The corpse shows no signs of decomposition: the reddish-brown fur is sleek and luscious, and there is no aroma of putrefaction. But the fox is definitely dead. Its eyes are slightly open and a delicate, milky sheen covers them, like a hint of cloud on a hot day.

The woman – elegant, well-groomed – remains motionless for a full minute. Then she phones the police. However, she finds it difficult to describe what has occurred, and to explain her predicament. The person to whom she speaks is reluctant to connect her with a police officer, as no crime appears to have been committed. The young woman gets angry. Eventually she is put through to an officer, who offers sympathy but confirms, regretfully, that this does not appear to be a matter for the police. Paradoxically, the woman is offered a number to contact a unit that provides support for victims of crime.

She sits on the floor in the doorway of the bedroom. She phones her ex-partner, who works at an advertising agency. He doesn't answer. Who answers the phone these days? He is thirty-five, two years older than her, and they broke up six months ago. She leaves a message, asking him to call her. She also sends a text to the same effect.

The woman goes to her kitchen and collects rubber gloves, plastic trash bags, disinfectant, cleaning materials. She returns to the bedroom, and tries to act swiftly, without thinking. The fox is not particularly large. A small-to-medium sized fox. The woman lifts the corpse, and finds it to be light, relative to her expectations. She places it into a trash bag, which she places in another, and another, which she seals with tape. The body leaves no trace, except a slight indentation in the deep weave of the carpet, which begins to vanish. Nonetheless, the woman cleans that area of the carpet assiduously.

She takes the bagged corpse to the trash chute in the marble lobby outside the door of her apartment. She is relieved to find the bag fits into the chute – just – without her needing to force it, or shove it, or exert any pressure on it. She listens as the bag tumbles down the chute. She doesn't really know where it goes. Probably into one of the large, wheeled bins she occasionally glimpses being serviced when she parks in the basement.

She takes a bath, and finds herself weeping. She goes to bed, in the guest bedroom.

Early the next morning her ex-partner phones. She describes finding the dead fox, and disposing of it, but he can't seem to grasp what she's telling him. She gets angry. He says he has to leave for work. She says must leave for work too. He says he will visit her after work, and maybe they can figure this thing out, whatever it is. She agrees.

That evening as she returns from work her ex-partner arrives at the same time. They were in a relationship for two years, and they bought the apartment together. It was a financial investment, they agreed, and she drew up a contract. Towards the end of their relationship she discovered he was being unfaithful to her. They broke up, and she kept the apartment, buying him out for the cost of his original investment, rather than what his share was worth relative to the apartment's actual value, which had increased. She is a good lawyer. He is a so-called Creative in a rapidly-changing industry, who has only recently begun to understand that what he thinks of as his skills will soon be superseded by machine learning, and his work will be done by algorithms.

The woman shows him where she found the dead fox. He suggests they could retrieve the corpse from the trash, and take a look at it. She asks why. He says it would help him understand her story. She gets angry. She calls the doorman in the lobby of the apartment block, who tells her the trash is collected every Wednesday morning. She thanks the doorman, and tells her ex-partner the corpse will have been taken away that morning.

He asks her if it's possible – at all possible – that she imagined the whole thing. She gets angry. He apologizes and says maybe someone with a key to the apartment put the dead fox in her bedroom for a joke, or another reason. Did she give a key to anyone? Like, if she's in a relationship – not that it's any of his business – and gave a key to her lover.

She denies giving a key to anyone. She says maybe he still has a key, maybe he kept a copy after he moved out. He states, emphatically, that he gave her his keys when he moved out, and didn't keep a copy. She tells him to think carefully, to confirm he's sure about that. He asks if she's accusing him of lying. She says it wouldn't be the first time.

Aaand there it is, he says. She says damn right there it is, she could never trust him. He asks if it ever occurred to her that the whole reason he betrayed her trust – just once, only that one time – was because he was so sick of her expecting him to betray her that it was, like, a self-fulfilling prophecy? She tells him to leave, she's had enough of his bullshit, more than enough, way more than enough. Her voice is hoarse. He leaves.

The next day, Thursday, the woman has an appointment with her therapist. She tells him what happened. He asks how she feels about it. She tries to describe how she feels but she can't pin it down: her feelings are slippery, elusive, and if she's totally honest there's a certain sensation, mixed in with the slippery feelings, that she could call

41

excitement, if she wanted to describe it, but she doesn't. The therapist asks if she thinks all this is connected in some way with the pregnancy incident. He is referring to a time, lasting no more than a week, during which the woman thought she might be pregnant, but it turned out to be a false alarm. These events took place a month after she broke up with her partner. The woman sighs. The pregnancy incident? Jesus, it was months ago, it lasted a week, it wasn't a big deal, it turned out to be nothing, she's totally over it, and why does he keep bringing it up? It's like he wants her to admit to something, some kind of trauma, even though it didn't happen, is that it? Okay, she says, I was devastated not to have an adorable little baby whose father was a total piece of shit, boo hoo. The therapist suggests they should, perhaps, do some work on her anger issues. She says nothing. She shakes her head slowly. He waits. She stands up and leaves. Her time was nearly up anyway.

The woman spends the next day feeling disconnected from her work, and watches TV in the evening. Everything seems equally unimportant, but equally interesting.

Early on Saturday morning the woman goes for a run in the park. She feels alert. She passes an unkempt man sitting on a bench and laughing quietly as he gazes around, shaking his head. He looks like a homeless person, and is possibly deranged. His clothes are drab, except for a red jacket, of the type, perhaps, worn by an entertainer who works on a cruise ship, or at an old-fashioned holiday camp, and she wonders if this man had such a job, and kept the jacket, which seems to fit him.

The man yells something at her as she passes: a strange, yodeling cry. She looks away quickly and runs on.

Ahead of her on the path she sees an elderly woman stumble and fall. She sprints to the old woman and helps her to her feet, and leads her to a bench. The old woman isn't hurt. She stumbled, she says, because there was a spot where the path was uneven. She smiles. Her face is wrinkled, but her eyes are clear and bright. The young woman asks her companion if she's sure she's all right. She feels her wrist being grasped by a hand with a surprisingly powerful grip. I'm all right, the old woman says, but what about you? She releases the young woman's wrist, and asks her to stay for a while, and unburden herself of whatever is troubling her. The old woman says she can tell something is wrong.

The young woman, for reasons she doesn't understand, finds herself describing the events of the last few days. The old woman doesn't appear to be surprised by the story of the dead fox. She says she knows about these things, and that they're caused by turbulent feelings, locked in the heart. The young woman laughs, but not with mirth. Don't try to tell me, she says, that it's about anger; that the dead fox is some kind of symbol, or a sign, or a manifestation of anger. Don't talk to me about anger issues. The old woman shakes her head with a smile. At this moment a group of cyclists flashes past. A dozen riders in tight formation, focussed and intent, their movements synchronised. A silent flock. Their clothing and the quality of their equipment indicate the seriousness with which they take their activity. In an instant they are gone, wheeling away around a curve.

The old woman watches them disappear. She turns to face the young woman again with an expression of tender amusement. She tells the young woman the fox has nothing to do with anger. It's love. The fox is the young woman's love, come to ask forgiveness. The young woman begins to laugh, but checks herself. She realises she is convinced that what the old woman is telling her is the truth; perhaps her matter-of-fact manner is what makes her so persuasive. The young woman is surprised to find tears on her cheeks. The old woman takes no notice of the tears. She says the young woman must perform a special ritual at the spot where she found the dead fox, to forgive her love. The old woman produces a bunch of herbs and presses them into the young woman's hand. She instructs her to burn the herbs – in a bowl or a dish, it's not important – and as the herbs burn she must open her heart and ask her love to forgive her. If she does this, all will be well. If not, the consequences will be grave. The young woman nods. There is nothing more to say. She stands, turns, and jogs away, gradually increasing her pace.

But the further she gets from the old woman, the more doubts she has. It's as if she's emerging from a trance. What was she thinking? At various times in the past she's been interested in this kind of thing – what she thinks of as spiritual stuff – but she always realises eventually that she isn't that type of person. The herbs in her hand are damp with perspiration. She throws them in a trash bin, and puts on more speed. She extends her usual route. She wants a long, hard run. She wants to outdistance everything, including herself. She arrives back at her apartment forty minutes later feeling exhausted and purged. She pulls off her top as she walks to the bedroom, and as she frees her head from it she stops in the doorway. On the carpet at the foot of her bed lies a fox. The same fox. She doesn't move. The fox appears to be breathing.

Tommy the Voice

Technology changes quickly, and it wasn't so long ago that the average person had a phone in their home but not in their pocket. These days, of course, you jump out of your skin if your landline rings – if you've even got one at all – and it's usually your mother, or a sweaty stranger reading from a script, trying to mislead you.

We're all accustomed to carrying phones around with us now, but the idea that we can use them to obtain pretty much anything we want, when we want it, is still relatively recent. A ride home in someone's car, for instance, summoned by an app. How long have we been able to do that? Not as long as you probably think. Only a few years ago, the streets of Britain were still riddled with minicab offices, crammed into impossible little cubby-holes next to train stations, and dilapidated storefront offices in which protective wire mesh was a big feature. A lot of those places were barely legitimate, and the later at night you found yourself in them, the weirder and dodgier they seemed. It was another time, in a different world, and it's where this story begins.

*

Outside, the streets of Clapham were cold, dark and wet but the minicab office blazed in a fluorescent Saharan noon, battering the retina and throwing every flap of peeling wallpaper into pitiless relief. It was two in the morning and I'd been at the counter for fifteen minutes, waiting for the car that the controller had promised me in five. I didn't feel like sitting on the bench by the window: almost all of its cracked, red upholstery was occupied by a very drunk kid with bad skin and a funny haircut. He was interfering with a wrapper of fish and chips, occasionally jabbing a crab-like hand into the soggy pouch and raising a clump of food to his mouth. He dropped most of it on the way, but some of it made it in there, where some of it stayed and some fell out again, cascading down the front of his shirt and on to the floor, or the bench, or back into the wrapper. It was a bit like watching one of those cruel amusement arcade games in which a mechanical claw grabs a prize but drops it before it reaches the chute.

Behind the sliding glass partition the controller leaned into her microphone. 'Seven-four, seven-four… come in, seventy-four… speak to me, Derek.' A squawk of static-riddled jabber erupted from a tinny loudspeaker. It seemed to satisfy the controller: 'Lovely, seven-four, tell me when you're clear.' From somewhere in the back came the percussive burp of an expertly-played video game. The controller's telephone rang. She picked up the receiver and adopted a tone of courtesy so insincere it amounted to mockery.

'Hello, car service… ah, yes, sir, Mr Draycott… Drayton, yes, you're waiting for your car from Hammersmith… yes, we're running a few minutes late on that… oh, that long, is it? Sorry about that, sir… alright, there's no need for that attitude, mate… no, because I've just spoken to the driver and he's approaching you now. The problem was, he couldn't find you because you're in the crack… the crack between the pages of the A to Z…' The controller looked up at me and winked.

I don't know why she thought I was on her side rather than the customer's. Maybe she thought my complicity would invalidate any complaints I might have as a customer myself. Or maybe she could tell I'd had a couple of drinks. Although I was nowhere near as drunk as the kid on the bench.

'No, not in yours, no,' she continued into the phone, 'we use a special edition in the trade… yes, he'll only be a minute or so now… yes, that's number three, Archer road, got that… alright, sorry for the delay, sir… yes, he's just at the end of your road now… thank you.'

The Controller replaced the receiver and leaned into her microphone again. 'All cars, all cars, anyone Hammersmith area? We got a screamer in Hammersmith. Anyone Hammersmith…? Anyone Hammersmith or Shepherd's Bush…? Anyone west of the Park…? Anyone west London…? Anyone London, for fuck's sake? Come on, speak to me you tossers!'

There was another sudden burst of incomprehensible crackling from the speaker. The controller raised her eyes theatrically and responded.

'Hello, one-five, I thought you was dead. Got a job for you.'

More noise from the speaker.

'No, forget your King's Cross regular, I've gave that to the ayatollah. Get yer arse over to… hang on… three, Ashley… no, Asquith… can't read it… Askey Road, Hammersmith. How long do you reckon, five minutes?'

I caught the words "bleedin' nightmare" in the crackling reply.

'Yeah, you'll do it in fifteen, easy. I'll tell him you're outside.'

The controller looked up at me thoughtfully, as if trying to place me. 'Oh, right, you want your car for Kentish Town, don't you?' She turned and bellowed over her shoulder, 'Lenny!'

Immediately, the video game stopped and a wiry little balding guy in a torn leather jacket sidled down the narrow passage at the side of the office.

'Alright, pal,' he muttered as he passed me, 'it's the blue Datsun.'

I got in the front and sat beside him. I wanted to say something about him being there in the back room all the time I was waiting, but I didn't think I could get the right tone.

'Alright?' I said, finally, to fill the silence as he heaved at the wheel to edge from a tight parking space.

'Alright for some, mate,' said Lenny, somehow managing to imply I'd offended him, 'but I tell you, this minicab driving is a mug's game, really.'

'Oh, yeah, tell me about it,' I said, tuning my accent down so it was a bit closer to his own Cockney, 'I've been in this game myself. Years ago.' It was true, but I'd only done it for about three months, and although that was plenty of time to experience the unpleasant aspects of the job, I wasn't exactly Travis Bickle. I wondered vaguely why I was trying to ingratiate myself. He was just one of those people who make you want their approval, I suppose. He didn't say anything. I was embarrassed now, and, just for something to say, I continued, 'But I always reckoned it was the controllers who've got the hardest job.'

He accelerated smoothly through an orange light at Queenstown Road and glanced at me thoughtfully. 'What do you do now, then?' he asked.

'I make most of my living as a writer.' I tried to make it sound like something only just inside the law.

'Oh yeah, a writer,' he said. Instead of asking me anything else he chewed his lip, made a controlled skid around the Vauxhall approach and swung out to pass a black Capri, the old JPS promotional model with gold lettering, once a flashy emblem of proletarian virility, now the badge of a loser so clueless he probably thought it was still cool, no irony. When the driver – a middle-aged guy with a mullet – realised he was being overtaken, he made a half-hearted attempt to speed up and aggravate us but he was too late. Lenny glanced into his rear-view mirror. 'Wanker,' he murmured affectionately, then he seemed to come to decision. 'You were a driver, yeah?'

'That's right,' I said, 'just for a while, it was back in–'

'Did you ever hear of Tommy the Voice, then?'

'I don't think so. I was a driver in Bristol, actually.'

'Oh, well, there you go.' He made it sound as if I'd admitted to a pitiful deficiency concerning my manhood. 'As it happens,' he continued charitably, 'Tommy the Voice was the best controller in the business. He was the Guv'nor, Tommy was. It's a gift, basically. I mean, you've been a driver, you know what it's like with some of them: leave you hanging about on the end of your rig, never get you the jobs, but Tommy was magic. Because it does take a certain type. It's like a general deploying his troops. You've got to know where all your drivers are, how long before they drop off, how long they're going to take to get to the next job, taking into account the traffic, time of day, weather conditions, everything. It's like one of those Russian geezers playing chess with twenty different people at the same time.' He took an unfamiliar turn after going over Vauxhall bridge but seemed confident enough, heading through Pimlico in the right general direction.

'Never mind all these black-cab drivers with the Knowledge and all that bollocks,' he said. 'I mean, I respect all that, but Tommy knew more about London traffic than any man alive. It's like he could sense things. He was like a crafty old spider in the middle of his web, picking up on every little tremble. A driver calls in: snarl-up on the Edgware road. So Tommy sends the car that's just dropped off in Kilburn down to a job at Euston, going via Regent's Park to miss the jam, and re-directs the one that's approaching Marble Arch from the Notting Hill end to go and pick up an account job due for half an hour in Battersea. Forward planning. Strategy. Tactics. Ever heard of a bloke called Orde Wingate? He was your man in World War Two: if you want creative strategic thinking applied with tactical flair, you study the Burma campaign, mate. Where was I? Oh, yeah. Another thing: Tommy didn't do drugs, like some of these controllers, speed freaks a lot of them; not that I've got anything against it necessarily, just that Tommy didn't need it.'

I realised where we were when we sailed around Hyde Park corner and he pointed the nose of the car up Park Lane with the rear end swinging behind us in a lazy pendulum. 'Why didn't you use Chelsea Bridge?' I asked.

'Roadworks. Anyway, Tommy the Voice was just one of those people you want to listen to. Like, some people are good with animals, Tommy was good with drivers. And it was all in the voice. Very relaxed, always in control. Like an airline pilot when they don't want you to worry, know what I mean? And that all goes back to this guy Chuck Yeager, as it happens, that way of talking. Do you know that book called The Right Stuff?'

'About the astronauts. By Tom Wolfe.'

'That's right, yeah,' he said, sounding pleased, 'have you read it?'

'I've seen the film.'

'Oh. Anyway, Chuck Yeager was the test pilot for the first American jets. Did they have that bit in the film?'

'Yes, he was played by Sam Shepard.'

'Really? Interesting actor. Playwright, and all. But it was Yeager who started all that casual style. You know, "Houston, we have a problem..." all of that. Quietly understated, you might call it. And the astronauts picked it up from him, and from them it went to the airline pilots. You know, the way they come over all smooth and soothing on the intercom: "Ladies and gentlemen, we're approaching a little spot of turbulence up ahead..."' Lenny said, doing a very passable imitation of a suave British pilot, 'when what they really mean is they're flying straight into a fucking hurricane and the engines have packed up. To be honest, there's a bit of showing off going on there, isn't there? About how cool they can be. Same with the minicab controllers. But no one could do it like Tommy the Voice, you've got to hand it to him.'

'Is he still working, then?' I asked. I realised I wasn't following our route any more, and now, looking out into the night, I couldn't tell where we were. Somewhere up behind Lisson Grove, I thought, although it's not the way I would have gone.

'No, he died years ago. Ten, twelve years. Interesting story, as a matter of fact. He turned out to be his own worst enemy, like a lot of them.'

'Who, controllers?'

"No, great men, leaders, that type of person. Achilles heel, feet of clay, know what I mean? Look at Napoleon. Yeah, it all started to go wrong one Saturday afternoon.'

'For Napoleon?'

'Tommy the Voice, you clown. No, this particular Saturday it was Tommy's birthday; no-one knew exactly how old he was but someone had found out the date. It was very quiet, summer holidays, and a lot of the regular work was off. A couple of drivers were watching the racing on the telly in the front office because there was no walk-in trade to speak of, so Tommy didn't mind. One of the drivers was a bit of a hound for betting on the horses and he kept on at Tommy to have a flutter. The thing is, only a few of the older drivers knew about it, but Tommy had a serious gambling problem. By this time, he hadn't had a bet for years, but it's like alcohol or drugs, isn't it? You can kick the habit but you're always going to be an addict.'

As it happened, this was something I knew quite a lot about, but I wasn't trying to impress Lenny any more, and I doubt that my experience would have impressed him anyway. It didn't even impress me any more. So I just said, 'Very true,' and left it at that.

'Too right, mate. But this particular driver didn't know about Tommy's problem, and when he phoned in a bet, he insisted on putting a tenner on for Tommy as a birthday present. So, what's the worst thing that could have happened?'

'The horse won.' It was the easiest question in the world for me to answer.

'You got it. And that was it. Tommy was well and truly hooked again. Told this driver, Scottish bloke he was, to put the winnings on the next race. That was when a man phoned in for a car to take him and his pregnant wife to hospital. She was ten days overdue, so she was booked in to have the baby induced. But, for once, Tommy's mind wasn't on the job: the TV in the minicab office was showing the runners for the next race by now, and Tommy and this driver, Angus, I think his name was, they were discussing the nags, checking the form, watching the odds: all the ritual that addicts wrap around the main event.'

He shot me a glance. He knew that I knew all about it, I could tell. Maybe he'd been there himself. People like us send each other some kind of subliminal signal. But I just nodded, and Lenny continued:

'It was only just before the race was about to start that Tommy remembered this hospital job. So, with his attention on the horses, he simply radioed the driver who was nearest the pick-up. Who happened to be a new driver in his first week on the job. No experience at all.

Tommy sent him to pick the bloke and his wife up in Finsbury Park and when the driver asked him for the best way to Guy's Hospital, Tommy told him Highbury Corner, down to the Angel, over Old Street then down over London Bridge, said it was a doddle and left him to it. Now, you might say that nobody could have predicted what happened. But that's the whole point: Tommy could have, because normally he thought of everything. But now he was only thinking of one thing, wasn't he? And it was only when the driver called in to say he was stuck in thick traffic that Tommy realised he'd directed the guy down through Islington, which is always packed on a Saturday afternoon. So, with one eye on the race, which had just started, he told the driver to turn off and gave him a parallel route down through the City. Big mistake.'

We stopped at a red light, and when I recognised the deserted intersection I figured out that Lenny was weaving diagonally up through Maida Vale and St. John's Wood in a kind of tacking manoeuvre. He drummed his fingers on the wheel as we waited. 'Well, of course,' he said, 'an experienced driver might have been able to take up the slack when it all started to unravel. And maybe if Tommy had won again, on that second race, he'd have left it at that and got back on the ball. But probably not. If a gambler does well, he keeps betting because he's on a winning streak; and if he loses, he keeps betting because it stands to reason that his luck's about to change. But either way…'

He accelerated away a nanosecond before the lights changed, and left a pause for me to complete the sentence for him:

'He always keeps betting,' I said.

Lenny nodded gravely. 'Next thing,' he continued, 'the driver calls in to say he's stuck in a jam on Canonbury Road. Tommy remembers there's roadworks on the new one-way system all the way down to Shoreditch. Been there for weeks. Should have remembered before. Then the driver says the woman in the back has started bleeding, she's in pain, he thinks she's going to need a doctor. Tommy tells him not to panic and he'll work something out. But even then, it didn't really get his attention. The last race was about to start and he still hadn't picked a horse. Once he'd done that, he gave the driver instructions to get him out of trouble. Or so he thought, but he wasn't thinking straight. So he didn't realise that what he'd done by now, in effect, was to direct the driver around three sides of a square, so that now the car was trying to cross the same traffic jam it had been stuck in to begin with. Then things got really bad.'

Lenny paused for a moment. I had a strange urge to take over the story myself and steer it towards a happier outcome than the one I could see unfolding inside it like a malignant growth. Lenny took a deep breath and continued:

'The young driver says he's completely gridlocked now. He can't turn, he can't move, he can't do anything. And then he starts yelling down the rig, going spare. Says there's blood everywhere, he thinks she's having the baby. Tommy tries to think. He's back on the case now, but it's too late. What can he do? Call an ambulance? No, it wouldn't get through. He thinks some more. Reckons the only thing is to locate a medic somehow, and get him on a courier service motorbike. So he gets the drivers in the office to work on that, and meanwhile he puts a call out to all his drivers on the road, and other firms as well, anyone he can raise, and asks if someone can patch straight through to the gridlocked car with some emergency medical advice. But by now, the woman's gone into labour and she's haemorrhaging badly.'

We reached the big intersection at Swiss Cottage and I thought it would be obvious which way to go now but Lenny turned left off Adelaide Road, and began driving through dark, leafy streets of big, expensive houses and I was lost again. When he spoke again, his voice had perked up and I thought maybe the story wasn't going to end so badly after all.

'Then a doctor did get to the car – a passing pedestrian, as it happens. He went to work like a demon to try and deliver the baby. And all the time the radio channel's open, and the young driver's giving Tommy a running commentary and Tommy can hear everything that's going on in the background, the woman screaming and the husband freaking out, and he can't do a thing, he just has to sit there in the office and listen. Finally, Tommy hears the cry of a new-born baby. The driver breaks down in tears and you can hear a bit of cheering in the background. But then it all goes quiet. Tommy keeps asking what's happening. The driver won't tell him, or can't bring himself to. Eventually he gets it out of him: the baby's still alright but the mother has died.'

We crossed Haverstock Hill just above Chalk farm and I knew where we were again now. It was the home stretch.

'That was the beginning of the end for Tommy the Voice. Once it had sunk in, he blamed himself for everything, of course. He carried on working but people said he'd lost his touch. He started working shorter hours and only did day shifts. And his voice changed. Didn't have the same ring to it, it was thinner, a bit hesitant. The confidence was gone, I suppose. And then, exactly a year later, Tommy was working a Saturday afternoon. It was very busy, there were a couple of big football games on and part of the Northern Line was shut down, as well. But Tommy wasn't really on top of it. Then he starts to get a bit distant, almost a bit dreamy. Starts asking who's heading west, is anyone on the Westway, anyone leaving town, driving into the setting sun. He gets slower and slower. And all over London, all his cars were slowing down. Because the controller keeps the whole network moving, keeps it alive. But what was happening was that Tommy's heart was giving out. They talk about arterial roadways, don't they? And all his cars out there were like little corpuscles, getting more and more sluggish, just like the blood that Tommy's heart was trying desperately to pump through his veins. He put up a terrific fight, but it couldn't last. Finally, the whole network of cars flowing through the city ground to a halt. His last message was, "All cars, stay in position." And that was the end of Tommy the Voice.'

We sat in silence for a while. Kentish Town Road. Nearly there.

'What happened to the driver?' I asked.

'What do you mean?'

'The young driver. Did he give up the job?'

There was a long pause while Lenny stared straight ahead without replying. Finally he shook his head, 'No,' he said. 'He kept at it. He's still driving.' There was another long pause. Lenny cleared his throat and when he spoke again he sounded glad to move on:

'Not quite the end of the story, as it happens. One week later, Saturday afternoon, you'd have had a hard time getting a minicab in west London. And even if you'd found one, you might have got stuck in very slow traffic. There was a cortege of minicabs over a mile long for Tommy's funeral. It was wonderful, magic. The vicar had been a driver at one time and he devised a special prayer made up of minicab patter; it was something like, "We beseech you, the controller of all things, to send your top driver, the Lord, to pick up a very special fare on account, and when you're POB, take our friend and brother Tommy the Voice to his well-earned bonus, dropping off at thy base in heaven…" that sort of thing. Everyone loved it.'

Lenny swung across the main road to make the turn to my address. 'But the funny thing was,' he continued, as he glanced at the house numbers, 'that his wife turned up. None of us even knew he was married. And you know what she told us? Tommy had never driven a car in his life. Never even took his test. In fact, he fucking hated cars.'

He pulled up neatly right outside my house. We sat in silence for a moment then I roused myself.

'What's the damage?' I asked, fishing out my wallet.

Lenny frowned at the steering wheel as if perplexed by some novelty in the concept of payment for the ride. He pursed his lips and finally he said, quietly, 'That'll be twenty-eight pounds fifty.'

'Christ,' I muttered, 'that's a bit over the odds, isn't it?'

'Well,' he said, 'I'm charging you a bit extra for the story. Because you'll probably use it.'

'What story?' By this time I was out of the car, handing three tens through his open window and making it clear with a gesture that I didn't want change.

'That story about Tommy the Voice that I just made up. You didn't believe all that old bollocks, did you?'

I just stood there with my mouth open for a moment. Then I shook my head, expelling a snort of what would have been laughter if it hadn't been mixed with more than a touch of bitterness. 'As a matter of fact,' I said, 'I did, yes.'

'Good,' Lenny said, 'and just remember, you're not the only writer who's worked as a minicab driver. Goodnight, mate.'

His electric window sliced up and he spun the wheel, raising one hand from it to wave briefly without looking back at me as he executed a smooth U-turn, clearing the cars parked on the other side of the road with a millimetre to spare, and surged away, back towards the lights of Kentish Town Road. I searched in my pocket for my keys.

I wondered why I was suddenly feeling lonely.

Warts

'Wait,' Luke said, 'how long ago was all this happening?'

The old man blinked. 'Still happens, according to some people.'

'But within living memory, right? I mean, you used to know people who'd done it, didn't you?'

'Aye. I've told you before.'

'I know, but I just wanted to establish a time frame for Nerissa.'

Luke's grandfather turned to the girl and smiled, revealing weirdly perfect dentures. 'He wants a time frame, does he? I'm not sure I've got one of them. I've always made do with a watch.' He winked at her.

Nerissa laughed. 'Me too,' she said, raising her wrist.

'I'll tell you what it is,' the old man said, leaning towards her in his bed, 'he doesn't trust us. He thinks you won't believe me, and you'll conclude I'm pulling your leg. Either that, or I've lost my marbles.'

Nerissa laughed again. 'I'll believe you, Mr Sykes, I promise.'

'Hey, we'll have none of that!' he cried, falling back against his pillows, pretending to be shocked. 'Mr Sykes was my dad! You can drop all that nonsense and call me Brian, if you please, young lady.'

'All right, Brian,' she said gravely.

'Thank you. Now, what were you saying when we were so rudely interrupted?'

Nerissa flashed Luke a grin before turning back to his grandfather. 'I wanted to ask you, do you think people genuinely believed that the wart man was a real person? Or was it more, you know, symbolic?'

'The older folk believed he was real. People like my grandparents, they knew he was real, no doubt about it. Once they'd paid their penny to the chemist, and he'd written a name down in the book, he'd say, Very well, Mrs So-and-So, the wart man is due on Tuesday week, and your lad's warts will be gone by the Thursday. And Mrs So-and-So would happily trot off home, knowing that little Tommy's warts would be gone in a fortnight, because the wart man would be along to take them away.'

'So you didn't even have to be there when the wart man came?'

'Oh, no. It was enough to know that he'd see the name in the book.'

'And what did he do – the wart man – when he saw the name?'

'The story was that the chemist would leave him alone with the book, in a back room, or somewhere. And after a while he'd give it back, and that was it.'

'But what do you think he did?'

Brian chuckled. 'Well now, I don't know whether an actual chap came along to the chemist's one dark evening, and employed some kind of strange power. The important thing is that folk believed he did. And some still do.'

'By the way,' Luke said, 'he means a pharmacist. When he says chemist.'

'Hey!' Nerissa frowned in mock annoyance and slapped his arm. 'Do you mind? I know what he means, thank you. I've lived here for three years, dude!'

The old man shook his head. 'I don't know why you put up with it. You're too good for him.'

Nerissa giggled. 'Maybe you're right, Brian!'

'Immature, that's his problem. You need an older man, Nerissa.' He winked at her again.

Luke sat back. He loved it when Brian flirted with his girlfriends. Afterwards they always told him how much they adored his grandfather, and what a wonderful character he was. And it certainly made the visits themselves more tolerable for Luke. In the two years since Brian had been in the care home he'd only visited by himself once. The other times had always been with a girlfriend. Nerissa was the third one Brian had met.

Now she was gazing into Brian's pale blue eyes and smiling. Luke knew his grandfather couldn't see her very well, especially as he refused to wear his glasses on these occasions. But Luke was confident the old man could see Nerissa well enough to register that she was very pretty. And that she was mixed-race, of course, which he probably found exotic. He'd spent most of his life in Huddersfield, and as far as Luke could tell he'd never shown much interest in the black and Asian families that had become a majority in the old working-class area where he'd still been living until he moved to the home.

'So, tell me, Brian,' Nerissa said, 'how do you think it works?'

'That's a good question, lass.'

He called her lass! Luke could have kissed him. He knew Nerissa would be tickled by it, and by everything old-fashioned and folksy about Brian.

More importantly, it would tell her something about Luke, and his roots. A bit of gritty credibility was a big advantage in his world, especially when it came to impressing actresses like Nerissa. There was always a moment in rehearsals when he judged it a good time to reveal his passionate side as a director, and then he allowed traces of a Northern accent to show up in his voice, so people could see it was always there, beneath the surface – a quiet, brooding strength informing the keen intelligence, and making him stand out from the Oxbridge types who dominated the top jobs in theatre.

'Medical science won't tell you much about it,' Brian was saying now, 'but there's lots of things medical science can't really explain. And as I'm sure you know, warts have always been associated with witchcraft and supernatural goings-on.' He gave her a sly, sidelong glance. 'Especially in certain cultures.'

Luke felt a coldness in his stomach. Christ, was the old man being racist?

Nerissa didn't seem to notice. 'Tell me about it!' she said. She widened her eyes comically. 'My great-granny, back in Saint Kitts, thought everything was a sign of witchcraft, or voodoo, or whatever. Any kind of mark on the body, and whoa, you're doomed to perdition, as far as she was concerned.'

'Extra nipples,' Brian said.

'Oh yes,' Nerissa said, 'those are much more common than most people realise. Which makes it easy if you want to prove someone's a witch. Although supernumerary nipples are authentic breast tissue, whereas warts are viral.'

Luke was getting creeped out. He didn't want to hear his grandfather and Nerissa talking about nipples.

'That's right,' Brian said. 'The human papilloma virus, which causes an extra layer of keratin to form on the top layer of skin.'

'Perhaps that partly explains the wart man,' Nerissa said. 'People in the old days must have known that you could catch warts, even if they didn't realise it consciously. And something that can be caught can also be set free, as it were.'

'A very apt metaphor, young lady,' Brian said. He pursed his lips and nodded slowly. Nerissa smiled at him and folded her arms.

Luke got the impression he'd just witnessed some kind of challenge being played out, a game he didn't understand. He looked at his watch, sighed, and pushed his chair back from the bedside, scraping its legs on the floor.

Nerissa was silent in the car, gazing out of the passenger window.

Luke drummed his fingers on the steering wheel. Eventually he said, 'What did you think of him?'

'Interesting man,' she said, without turning from the window.

Luke waited for her to say something about Brian's charm, or his eccentricity, but she didn't.

'You okay?' he said.

'Sure. I'm fine.'

Luke found it difficult to read her signals sometimes. Like the first time he slept with her. Afterwards he told her he'd wanted to go to bed with her ever since he'd set eyes on her, but he waited until the production was up and running, and his job as a director was done, because of the ethical implications. He said he was aware of all the issues around abusive power relationships, and how tough it was for women in that situation, with a director in a position of authority, especially for a younger actress and a slightly older guy with a relatively high status. She just laughed. 'I would have fucked you on the first day, if you'd asked,' she said.

As Luke swung the car onto the motorway slip road he tried again. 'That stuff about the wart man. Pretty extraordinary, right?'

Nerissa was checking her phone. She glanced up at him. 'Yes, fascinating.'

'Amazing story, and I'd love to do something with it. Maybe develop a show of some kind. The Wart Man. You know, like a superhero. Wartman! He rids the world of warts! An ironic superhero. Maybe a musical. What do you think?'

'Are you into all that?'

'What, musicals?'

'No, folklore. Superstitions.'

'Sure, of course. But I'm talking about the general idea of a stage show.'

Nerissa shrugged. 'It depends how it's done, I suppose. I'm sure you've been thinking about it for a while. It's not the first time he's told you the story, is it?'

'No, I've heard it before. Several times. He's entering his anecdotage, as they say.'

'But you still wanted me to hear it.'

'I just thought you'd find it interesting.'

'Why? Because of the cultural angle?'

Luke was taken aback. Shit, he thought, is she implying that I'm being racist? God, she was confusing sometimes. 'Not at all, I just meant—'

'Or the gender factor, because a woman must know about witchcraft, and warts, and all that shit?'

'I honestly wasn't thinking about it.'

'Actually, there's a title for your show. Women, Warts and Witches. You can have that for free.'

Luke realised she'd probably been teasing him. 'Thanks,' he said, 'I'll give you a credit.'

'And Brian, I assume. It's his story, after all.'

'It's not really his story. It's folklore, like you said.'

Nerissa laughed. 'That's what a story is! It's what someone tells you.'

Luke tried to suppress his irritation. 'But what I mean,' he said, 'is that I'd develop it. Into something with a life of its own. You know, with a different life.'

Nerissa put her hand on his knee. 'Don't worry, baby.' She slid her hand up to his crotch and rested it there lightly. 'Don't overthink these things.' She removed her hand and turned her attention back to her phone.

Three weeks later Luke was having sex with an actress called Brigitte when he felt her freeze momentarily as they were both approaching a climax.

He raised his head. 'What's up?'

She smiled at him brightly. 'Nothing. Keep going!' She thrust her hips up encouragingly, but Luke noticed she didn't replace her hands on his back, which she'd been clutching tightly. Instead she twined her fingers into his hair and kept them there until they both came.

After she'd left Luke's flat – it was mid-afternoon, and she had an evening waitress shift in a local gastro-pub – he brought his shaving mirror into the bedroom and used it with the mirror on the wall to inspect his back. There were four small growths near the base of his spine. They felt surprisingly prominent to his touch.

He'd never had warts before, but what else could they be?

No wonder Brigitte had reacted the way she did, although she'd concealed it well, being an actress. It was the second time they'd fucked, and Luke wondered how long the warts had been there. Maybe she hadn't noticed them that first time. They'd both been pretty drunk.

Perhaps he should talk to her at rehearsals tomorrow, and reassure her that he didn't have warts anywhere else – which he didn't:

he checked carefully. He wished he hadn't broken his rule about sex with actresses he was working with, but his confidence had taken a knock when Nerissa dumped him – shit, it was years since that had happened to him! – and besides, Brigitte was nearly the same age as him. He decided to wait and see if she mentioned anything.

Rehearsals were nearly over, and for the next few days he was scrupulously polite to her. She behaved as though nothing had happened between them, which suited Luke.

There were some glitches in the tech run, and the dress rehearsal was a little shaky. But the press night was good. A triumph, people said. However, he decided not to go to the party afterwards.

A week later Luke noticed two warts on the upper part of his right arm. The next day there was one on his other arm, close to his wrist.

He went to his doctor. She confirmed that the growths were warts, and gave him some cream to put on them, and told him to come back in two weeks if there was no change. She said it was unusual for warts to make their first appearance on the lower back, but warts were unpredictable. She told him to be careful about hygiene, which he found frankly insulting.

As he applied the cream that night he noticed a wart at the top of his breastbone, almost on his neck.

More warts appeared in the next two weeks. He began to feel angry with the doctor. She'd seen him for less than ten minutes, and offered nothing more than ointment and platitudes.

But when he returned to see her his anger dissipated as she examined him, frowning and saying very little. She continued to frown as she consulted an online database, then flipped through a medical directory on her desk, and then looked in another, thicker volume which she took from a drawer.

Luke tried to conceal his desperation as he asked her what was wrong, and what could be done. She wrote him a prescription for a liquid to paint onto the warts every night, and said she was referring him to a dermatologist. He asked how long that would take on the NHS. She didn't know, exactly: a few weeks, perhaps? Luke allowed his exasperation to show. Couldn't she see it was an emergency? Apparently she couldn't, although she offered her sympathy.

Luke was hired to direct an Ayckbourn revival in Guildford. It wasn't his usual type of work, but the producers said they wanted someone to bring an edgy vibe to it. The money was pretty good, and it would only take four weeks. He found one of the actresses in the cast extremely attractive, and made his interest clear to her, discreetly, but he was careful not to do anything about it. He resolved to wait until his involvement with the production was over – by which time his warts would be gone, he hoped.

The new treatment wasn't working, and now a couple of warts were visible on his throat. He decided to see a dermatologist as a private patient. He was able to book an appointment with a specialist within two days.

The man's office was in an elegant house in Mayfair. He was in his sixties, well dressed and carefully groomed, and his clean, firm fingers touched Luke's skin with gentle confidence.

After he'd washed and dried his hands he smiled at Luke across a mahogany desk. He explained that Luke's warts were of a virulent type, but could be dealt with very effectively by a new dual therapy that had been developed specifically to tackle cases of this kind. It was a little more expensive than other treatments, but undoubtedly it would sort things out.

Luke left the specialist's office feeling relieved, and slightly foolish for having been so worried. After all, they were only warts.

*

He took to wearing a silk scarf, even though it was late April, and tried to carry it off nonchalantly. He wore long-sleeved shirts to conceal the warts on his arms, or a t-shirt with a light jacket which he didn't remove. There was nothing he could do about the growths that had appeared on the backs of hands. Wearing gloves would have attracted more attention than it deflected.

Two weeks into the Guildford job he got a call from his agent, asking him to come into the office. That was unusual. Luke hoped there was news about one of his long-term projects, perhaps from the American producer he'd been discussing things with.

But it turned out he was getting fired from the job in Guildford. His agent, Lucy, told him the theatre management had being having second thoughts about his approach. When Luke demanded more details she revealed, in confidence, that there was also a suggestion he'd behaved inappropriately. She reminded him it wasn't the first time. Luke didn't defend himself, but inwardly he fumed. He didn't believe the real reason for his dismissal was anything to do with his behaviour, or his artistic approach. He'd seen the way Lucy looked at him when he arrived in her office, having turned down the offer of lunch at a restaurant. He was wearing a high-necked sweater, and took care to conceal his hands, but he was convinced she'd heard about his condition.

He asked if she had any offers of work for him, or any news of his projects. She said she was sure there'd be something soon. When they said goodbye, and he moved in to exchange their customary kisses on the cheek, he was aware of an awkwardness in Lucy's response. Her lips barely touched his skin.

A wart appeared higher up his neck, just below his left ear. He revisited the specialist and found the man less congenial this time, with a trace of hostility beneath his urbane manner. He recommended hospital tests. When Luke heard how much this would cost, he said that he couldn't afford it, and he'd have to go back on the NHS to have the tests.

The specialist made it clear his interest in Luke was at an end. He said it was unusual for the condition to resist the treatment he'd prescribed, but Luke hadn't responded, which he regretted. But not enough to waive his fee, of course.

The next day Luke discovered a wart on his face.

*

He was surprised by how quickly his life fell apart.

By the end of June, he had no money in his bank account to pay the next month's rent on his flat in Hackney. He cashed his Premium Bonds, which were the only savings he had. He'd always assumed there would be plenty of time for that kind of thing later in his career, and it hadn't occurred to him that he might face the prospect of poverty before he was forty.

It was also a shock to discover how few friends he had. He'd never made a particular effort to cultivate friendships, but he had the impression there were plenty of people who liked him enough to want to spend time with him. Now he found there were only two people he could rely on for sympathetic conversation, and both lived abroad. One was an ex-girlfriend who was now a set designer in L.A., and the other was an acquaintance from his schooldays, Caspar, who'd moved to Sydney and did something in the insurance business. Luke had always treated him disdainfully, and suspected Caspar was in love with him. Whatever the reason for his loyalty, Luke was grateful for it now. He was vaguely aware that his calls sometimes roused Caspar from sleep.

For the first time in many years he found himself missing his mother, who had died when he was twenty, and she was forty-three. At the time she seemed to slip out of his life unobtrusively, having been diagnosed with ovarian cancer and succumbing sooner than was expected. His father began to drink even more heavily than he had throughout Luke's childhood, and was killed in a car accident two years later. Luke felt nothing for a man who'd been an absent figure at the best of times, and too present at the worst, but now he started dreaming about his mother, and sometimes he woke up in tears.

The only consolation was that the warts were no longer spreading so quickly. There were even times when he convinced himself they'd actually begun to retreat, only to discover that a new one had appeared overnight.

In the middle of August Luke got a call from the manager at his grandfather's care home. She said his condition had deteriorated, and asked Luke to visit.

'I didn't know there was anything wrong with him,' Luke said.

'There isn't, particularly,' she said, 'apart from living a long time.'

'Oh God, are you saying he's dying?'

'I'm just saying it might be a good idea to come and see him.'

'Yes, of course. I'll come on Monday.'

As Luke ended the call he was already calculating what the trip would cost him on the train. He no longer owned a car, and his only income was from writing reports on screenplays that Lucy sent him, some of which she diverted from other readers employed by the agency, knowing how desperate Luke was.

In the end he took a coach to visit his grandfather.

Luke scarcely recognised the shrunken figure in the bed. Death had already staked a claim to him. He was a ghostly tenant in his own body, waiting to be evicted.

'Hello, Gramps, Luke said. He hadn't called him Gramps for years.

Brian opened his eyes. They looked cloudy and opaque. 'Luke?'

'Here, Gramps.' Luke patted the bedclothes next to Brian's shrivelled hand. He didn't want to touch him.

The old man's eyes found him, then drifted across the room. A reedy whisper emerged from his lips. 'You by yourself?'

'That's right. Just popped in to see you. Are you all right?'

The corner of Brian's mouth twitched with the trace of a smile. He lowered his eyelids and raised them again slowly – as a kind of nod, Luke understood.

For a couple of minutes he listened to his grandfather's shallow breathing. He shifted in his chair. 'Oh, by the way, Gramps,' he said, startled by the loudness of his own voice in the hot little room, 'do you remember the last time we talked about that story of yours? The one about the wart man?'

Brian lowered and raised his eyelids again.

'I was interested,' Luke continued, 'when you said people still believe in it, and maybe there's even, like, someone still doing it? You know, a… wart man?'

Something seemed to sharpen in Brian's expression. His gaze became fixed on Luke's face.

Luke was sure the old man couldn't see him clearly, but reflexively he rearranged his scarf. 'I wanted to do a bit of research,' he said. 'For an idea I've got. Check a few things out. I mean, does it actually still happen? And if so, where? Where do people go?'

With a shock Luke felt the old man's hand on his wrist. It had shot out with surprising speed, and now his brittle fingers fluttered against Luke's skin. He knew Brian could feel the warts on his flesh. His grandfather opened his mouth wide, stretching a rope of spittle between his lips. He was trying to say something. His chest heaved.

Luke brought his head closer. 'What, Gramps?'

'Bollocks,' Brian gasped, and fell back.

That was the last word Brian spoke to him. He died a week later. Luke went to the funeral, which was attended by only three other people, two of whom were members of staff from the care home. The other was an elderly woman who claimed to be an old friend of Brian's. Luke got the impression she'd hoped, many years ago, to marry him.

Two weeks later a solicitor informed Luke that his grandfather had bequeathed him a house in Huddersfield.

Luke was amazed. He'd assumed the house had been sold long ago, to pay the fees for Brian's care, but it seemed the old man had squirreled away enough cash for that.

The next day, as he was still trying to absorb the news, Luke received the results of his hospital tests, which he'd finally undergone just before his visit to Brian. They were inconclusive. In other words, nothing could be done.

Luke went to Huddersfield. The small, dilapidated house stood at the end of a terrace in a run-down area. He had it valued, and confirmed his suspicion that it wouldn't fetch nearly enough to buy a place anywhere in London, even out in the suburbs. He could sell it, and live on the money, but for how long? He was facing eviction from his flat, and what he earned from the script consultancy work wasn't covering the rent, let alone other expenses. It would, however, be enough to live on if he moved out of London and had no rent to pay.

Why not? He had no social life. He spent his days indoors, and when he ventured out at night he shunned places where he would be seen by anyone whose reaction to his appearance he cared about.

He moved in.

*

Luke lived in the dark. He kept the curtains closed, and hardly noticed as the days got shorter. He was covered in warts. He walked the streets at night, muffled in an overcoat, scarf and gloves, with a cap pulled down over his eyes.

He knew he was neglecting himself and he suspected he was beginning to stink. What did it matter? The house next door was occupied by an elderly Asian couple who rarely ventured out. The next house along was used by drug dealers. Occasionally Luke wondered if he could get something from them to help him end his life. He spent a long time thinking about doing it, and knew he was serious about it, but a part of him refused to believe it was all over. While he was ready to acknowledge that his life had been useless, and everything he'd valued was shallow and frivolous, he couldn't accept that his fate was to die like this, alone and overlooked. It wasn't fair. He knew he'd done some good work, and on a few occasions he'd created real art.

He wanted to believe that his refusal to despair was down to strength of character, but he knew it was largely about egotism. It was interesting to get insights like that, although they didn't help much. But he kept going.

He caught a cold, which got worse. His chest began to rattle. He knew he should see a doctor but he couldn't face it.

One evening in late November he left the house and walked aimlessly, keeping up a fast pace, striding through the shadows. About a mile from the house he passed a chemist's shop with its lights still on. It was seven-thirty. A printed notice on the door announced late opening on Thursdays. Luke peered through the window and saw a young Asian guy in a white coat behind the counter. He decided to get the strongest cough medicine he was permitted to buy without a prescription. If nothing else it might help him sleep.

As the door closed behind him he froze. The words on the sign above the doorway he'd just walked through detonated in his mind. It was the name of the shop. Bullock's Pharmacy.

The young man behind the counter was staring at him, and Luke realised the scarf had slipped down from his face.

He allowed it to sink in. This was the place. His grandfather's final word to him reshaped itself. Luke had asked him where people went, when they still believed – and Brian had told him. Of course. It was bound to be a place like this, tucked away in a back street, only a mile from the house. An old family business, now run by Asians – but the way the pharmacist was looking at him gave Luke hope that the tradition was still alive. This was where he could be cured.

The young man stepped out from behind the counter. He stood in front of Luke, keeping his distance. 'It's you,' he said.

'What do you mean?'

'The wart man.'

'No,' Luke said, 'that's who I want. The wart man.'

The guy nodded slowly. 'They said you'd come.'

'How the fuck can I be the wart man? Look at me!' Luke unwound the scarf and tore the gloves from his hands, which he thrust towards the pharmacist.

The guy took a step back but kept his eyes fixed on Luke's. 'Yeah, that's right, bruv. Look at you.'

'I'm covered in warts!'

'Right. That's how it works, isn't it? You take them on.'

Luke heard a harsh wheezing sound. He realised it was him: he was breathing heavily through his mouth. He tried to understand the truth that was uncoiling inside him. This was his fate. The biblical Luke was a healer. But in the end it was Christ who took on the sins – the contaminations of this world.

The pharmacist retreated behind the counter and bent down behind it. He straightened up holding what looked like a biscuit tin. 'The money's in here.'

Luke laughed. Was the guy seriously going to give him a bunch of loose change? He stopped laughing when he saw inside the tin. Five, ten- and twenty-pound notes. A lot of them.

'There's two more shops in Huddersfield,' the pharmacist said, 'and one up in Bradford. And I've heard there's a couple in Leeds.'

Luke felt strangely calm. 'How often?' he asked.

The pharmacist shrugged. 'Once every two months or so. For each shop.'

'Where's the book?'

'Come around the back, bruv.' He moved aside so Luke could walk behind the counter. 'Wait there, and I'll get it for you. People were sure you'd come, and there's quite a backlog.'

'It's all right,' Luke said, 'I'm here now.'

A Very Nice Man

The woman opposite me was crying. I'd been engrossed in my book since the train had left Bristol but when I heard her snuffling I glanced up. She looked about forty and her face was pretty, even though her eyes were red and swollen. She was on the large side, and the sober business suit she was wearing seemed a little small for her. I noticed that her shoes had very high heels.

'Are you all right?' I said.

She nodded and blew her nose on the handkerchief she'd been dabbing her eyes with. 'I'm all right, thanks, love. Just been to a funeral, that's all.'

'Oh, I'm sorry,' I said. 'Was it someone close?'

'Not exactly. But he was such a nice man. Probably my best client.'

She must have seen the momentary calculation in my eyes as I glanced at her shoes again and took in the curves beneath her tight clothes. 'Oh, I don't care,' she said, 'I've got nothing to be ashamed of.'

'No, of course not,' I said, feeling ashamed myself now. To cover my awkwardness I blurted out, 'So… you liked him, then?'

She gave me a little smile and blew her nose again. 'Most of my clients aren't really any trouble, to be honest,' she said. 'You give them a bit of a massage, because that's what it says in the advert, but after a few minutes with the baby oil and a bit of chat, you get on with what they've really come for.'

She smiled again, and I smiled back. She had a soft, pleasant voice with a slight Midlands accent. 'I don't get many perverts,' she said, 'because I don't do much kinky stuff. But this client, he was a very nice man, and he wanted domination. You know, from a mistress. Not spanking or whipping, thank God, because that really makes your arms tired; no, he wanted me to make him scrub the kitchen floor. I had to pretend to be really cross with him and call him all kinds of names. Then I'd order him to scrub the floor. So, he'd start scrubbing, and I'd take the opportunity to nip out to the shops for half an hour. Trouble was, sometimes when I got back, I'd forget about the domination, and I'd go in the kitchen and he'd be there on his hands and knees, and I'd say, Ooh, that's lovely, that is, you've done a really thorough job, right into the corners, too! And then he'd look at me with a face like a robber's dog, and I'd have to say, No! Actually, your mistress is most displeased! You miserable worm, do it all again! And then he'd start all over again, happy as Larry.' She gave a little laugh and shook her head. 'That went on for ten years. Then he moved to Trowbridge to be the customer service manager in a big electrical store, dealing with all the complaints. I expect that kept him happy.'

'You must miss him,' I said.

'I do. He gave that floor a lovely clean every week, and paid me forty quid for the privilege. But most of all…' she turned and gazed out of the window for a moment, then said quietly, 'He was a very nice man.' She sighed, and then stood up. The train was pulling in to Swindon. 'This is my stop,' she said.

I ignored my book for the rest of the journey. I wished I'd spoken to her at the funeral service. She must have been at the back, and we hadn't seen each other. But I was grateful to her. I'd learned something I hadn't known about my late father. And she was right: he was a very nice man.

Sweet Prince

I dreamed of flies. Other insects too, but mostly plump, drowsy flies.

After the first time it happened I mentioned it to the princess in the morning as we lay beneath the furs. The sun was beginning to warm the room beyond the heavy drapes enclosing the huge oak bed. Nothing is less interesting than other people's dreams, but we'd been married only a year and we were still greedy for everything about each other.

'What happened in the dream?' she said.

I hesitated. She frowned at me with an expression of mock impatience.

'Not much of note,' I said. 'And you? Did you dream?'

'Yes, I had a dream.'

'What happened?'

Serena rolled towards me. 'I don't know.'

'What do you mean?'

'I'm still in the dream,' she said, beginning to caress me, 'so we shall have to see, won't we?'

I laughed, and we made love. As I say, we'd been married only a year.

Three nights later I had a similar dream. It was more vivid than the first, full of strange passions and frightening, half-glimpsed events, but the flies, when they appeared, were no match for me. In the morning, as I propped myself up against the pillows, the spirit of the dream lingered within me. I became aware that my wife was awake at my side. The golden drapes around the bed were beginning to glow, and I gazed into the muted intricacies of their tapestry. I didn't want to recount the visions to Serena.

'Another bad dream?' she said, and stroked my cheek. I took her wrist and turned it, and kissed the inside of it. As I moved my lips slowly up her arm she shuddered.

Later, as we were getting dressed, she spoke my name quietly:

'Anton.'

I paused in the act of buttoning my tunic. She was standing on the other side of the bed, still partly unclothed. The sight of her thighs above her hose aroused me instantly, and I would gladly have renewed the exertions that had ended a few moments earlier in our shouts of shared ecstasy. Seeing her like this in the morning never failed to stimulate me. In the early days of our marriage we were frequently late for breakfast.

Now her face was solemn. 'I don't want you to worry,' she said.

'What makes you think I'm worried?'

'I know you better than you know yourself, my prince.'

'Is that true? Well, if I wasn't worried before, I am now.'

She smiled, but it was plain she was not to be deflected by levity.

'Perhaps,' she said, slipping her shift over her head as her lady-in-waiting stepped forward with her robes, 'affairs of state weigh heavily upon you, as my father becomes increasingly… abstracted. Is that the right word, do you think?'

'Delicately put,' I said, 'and I cannot deny I am vexed, but only by my concern that your noble father may be suffering in his sorry condition.'

The princess sighed. 'The king does not suffer much, I believe, but he is often bewildered. I beg you, open your heart to me if you find your duties burdensome, Anton.'

I was fully dressed now, and I strode around the bed and took her in my arms. She softened into my embrace, but I held my lust at bay, and kissed her chastely upon her pale, freckled forehead.

'My love,' I murmured, 'I swear that if I am troubled I will open my heart to you, and you will, indeed, know me better than I know myself, troubles and all.'

I stepped back and allowed the lady-in-waiting to do her work. She was a strikingly pretty girl, from whom nature had withheld the power of both speech and hearing, and we were able to converse freely in her presence. As I left the room I treated her to my most charming grin.

As it happened, we had an appointment with the king that morning.

Serena and I entered the Lesser Hall, where the monarch held his more intimate audiences, and approached him hand-in-hand. It was the custom for the prince and princess to display this sign of harmony, but we would have done it in any case. We liked to hold hands.

The king was well advanced in years and the hoar frost was upon his hair and beard. I'm not speaking metaphorically. He was covered in frost, as a result of his insistence on bathing in the river every day as soon as he awoke. Although it was nearly springtime it was still bitterly cold in the early mornings, when the king would remove all his clothes and plunge into the icy water, gasping and whooping. When he was younger he took good care to dry himself after he emerged from the water, but now he was frequently to be seen – by people of all ranks – wandering along the riverbank stark naked, absently twining flowers and creepers into his beard and hair, including the hair around his private parts.

Sometimes he remained in this condition, hallooing cheerful greetings to his astonished subjects – who did their best not to notice his nakedness – until the sun began to climb. Occasionally I encountered him myself, when I was taking my morning swim, and he never failed to greet me politely.

Eventually his attendants would coax him into his clothes and back to the palace. By this time, however, the water on his person, and the dampness in his garments – which he left strewn about, forbidding anyone to touch them – would have frozen, with the result that he frequently held audience sparkling like an elderly sprite or snow-goblin.

He was losing his mind, of course.

As I approached him, I could see he didn't know me. This was the fourth or fifth failure of his memory in this respect, and these lapses were becoming more frequent. Even worse, there was a moment during our previous audience when it was apparent the king had forgotten who Serena was.

On this occasion, however, he smiled at her as she bowed to him, and nodded happily. Then he cast a glance at me.

'My dear,' he said to her, 'who is this lanky young fellow you have brought here, and why does he hold you by the hand so impertinently?'

The princess had learned by now that any attempt to correct her father's misapprehensions would be fruitless while his wits were addled. Nonetheless, she stepped forward, her hand still in mine, and smiled at him sweetly.

'Father,' she said gently, 'this is my husband, prince Anton.'

The king didn't appear to hear her, and he continued to gaze at me thoughtfully. 'He looks like a dog,' he said. 'Or a log, or a frog.'

My heart beat faster. I felt my wife squeeze my hand, and when I glanced at her I saw a tear in her eye. Naturally we were both distressed. In addition, the growing disorder of the king's mind could prove troublesome to me if he became convinced I was a rogue who had stolen his daughter from him, and intended to usurp him. There was a danger he would order his guards to seize me and confine me, or worse.

He regarded me now with a crafty smile. Not for the first time I wondered if he were dissembling in order to trick me. Yes, he was going mad, but he knew he was going mad, and he was quite capable of feigning madness, and play-acting, when it suited him. He was a cunning old madman.

Beside me the princess took a breath, and was about to reply to her father's remarks concerning me, when a figure appeared at the king's shoulder – from nowhere, it seemed – and leaned down to murmur in his ear. It was the chancellor, Lord Abel, and the king listened to him intently. He nodded, and when Lord Abel finished speaking the king addressed me:

'My dear son, prince Anton, please forgive me. I was out of sorts, but am recovered.'

Then he giggled like a child, which was most unsettling. However, I was reassured by the presence of Lord Abel, and so was my wife, who relaxed her tight grip upon my hand. The remainder of the audience passed uneventfully.

He was an extraordinary man, Lord Abel.

I had never met anyone so thoroughly contained within himself. I would estimate his age as fifty, and there was nothing very remarkable in his appearance save his clear grey eyes, which seemed exceptionally bright, like a steady, pale flame. His manner was friendly, and not once did I hear him raise his voice. Nonetheless, his advice was always heeded. I believe his complete command of himself gave him the power to command others, even the king.

I had many reasons to be grateful to Lord Abel. When my wife had asked me, earlier that morning, whether affairs of state weighed heavily upon me, she and I both knew the chancellor prevented those concerns from becoming burdensome to me. From the first moment I found myself at the court, and understood I was an emissary of my people, Lord Abel offered himself as a rudder to help me steer my course with the king, and he became an invaluable counsellor to me. With the settlement concluded, my duties became largely ceremonial. I greeted visiting dignitaries, and made sure their attendants were well supplied with the diversions such courtiers expected. They, in turn, offered me the respect my position demanded, for I was, after all, the prince.

The decline in the king's health added no weight to my obligations, because the chancellor took it upon himself to spare me any discomfort. Abel was energetic, wise, and powerful. He pursued the fulfilment of his wishes relentlessly, and would go to any lengths, with unfailing courtesy, to eliminate opposition to them.

The following day my wife informed me she was with child.

We celebrated by passing the afternoon in bed, exhausting one another.

My dreams began to fill with water. I felt a distance opening within me, between the languid daytime pleasures of a mild spring, and the nights in which I thrashed and gulped through clouded, churning liquid. I began to mistrust my judgment.

One morning, with the princess in my arms, I asked her to tell me again the story of how she saved my life.

She raised herself onto her elbows and looked down at me.

'Again?'

'I never tire of it,' I said.

'Very well. Sit up, arrange those pillows behind my back, take my hand, and I shall tell you the story. Again.'

When we had settled ourselves, she began.

'I was hunting in the forest,' she said, 'and my blood was up. For many days I'd been expecting – with deep displeasure – the arrival of a suitor. I knew nothing of him, save that he was a prince in his own land beyond the sea, that he was coming to conclude a treaty with our kingdom, and that my father had ordered me to look favourably upon him. Naturally, I despised him. Who was this youth, to believe he had a right to take my hand in marriage? And not because he desired me – no, I was merely a convenient adjunct to a diplomatic manoeuvre! I was determined to refuse him, and to defy the wrath of my father, and anyone else who cared to tax me on the matter.'

I laughed. 'Heaven help the man who taxes you.'

'Be quiet. I'm telling the tale. So, I was riding like the devil. I outstripped my attendants, even the guards who were supposed to keep me out of harm's way. I left them far behind me as I rode deep into the woods, hot and reckless. I could hear them in the distance, calling my name, cursing the forest, complaining they were lost, until even their voices faded, and I was alone.

'Then I saw it. A body – a corpse, as first I thought – lying half-submerged in a stream. I reined in my horse, sprang down, and summoned all my strength to drag the body from the water and onto the bank.

'I saw it was a young man: tall, well-proportioned, with dark hair and a pale countenance – oh, so very pale. Pale unto death. There was a gash upon the forehead, caused, I surmised, by a blow that had robbed the young man of his senses, and perhaps of his life, for who knew how much time he'd spent with his head and most of his body in the freezing water?

'Nothing daunted, I rolled the man onto his back, as I'd been taught. I pinched his nose, opened his mouth, and made sure there was no obstruction lodged in his throat. Then I covered his mouth with mine.'

The princess paused and glanced at me. 'Why do you shake your head?'

'I am still amazed,' I replied, 'by what you did. Where I came from, such arts were unheard of, and if they had been known, they would never have been taught to a woman.'

'Be grateful that they were, to me, by good Doctor Bowl. We are both fortunate I had such a skilled physician to instruct me. And thus I preserved your life, by sealing your mouth with my lips, and blowing my breath into you, until you gave a spasmodic jerk, then another, then sat bolt upright and violently spewed a quantity of water from your gullet.'

'And looked into your eyes,' I said, 'and was lost.'

'Shall I go on?'

'Yes. I remember nothing of what happened.'

Serena kissed my cheek. 'Nothing? Even now?'

I shook my head. 'I recall my recovery, here in the palace. But before that, all is still darkness. You must tell me my own story.'

'Very well. Finally, my attendants, breathless and astonished, found us. We brought you here, and as they carried you inside we heard a shout. An adjutant to Lord Abel ran to us, and exclaimed that we had found the prince! The officer had visited your kingdom three years before, as a member of the first diplomatic mission, and he recognised you. Just moments earlier he had been conveying to Lord Abel reports that had reached him, of the events that led to you being discovered, alone and half-dead, deep in the forest.'

'It was because,' I said, 'my party was set upon by marauders, and there was a fierce battle.'

'They were Mountain People,' the princess said, 'and all your companions were killed by them, or carried off to servitude.'

'And I alone survived by riding into the forest. Riding like the wind.'

'Yes, deep into the forest, where the Mountain People fear to go. And there your steed must have stumbled, and you fell into the stream.'

'And what became of that trusty steed?'

'No one knows.'

'A pity. I would have liked to thank her for her noble service to me.'

'My love!' my wife exclaimed, causing me to start. Her eyes were shining with excitement. 'You say she was a mare! And you have never said that before!'

I frowned. 'Truly?'

'Yes!' cried Serena. 'Is it possible, my dear Anton, that you begin to recall, for yourself, what took place?'

I made no reply to this, puzzling over what I'd said. Was it a chance conjecture, or was the shroud that lay over my past beginning to lift?

'Please do not distress yourself,' Serena said, stroking my arm. 'Whether your memory of this dark time returns to you or not, nothing will alter our happiness. And now, shall I conclude the story?'

I nodded and lay back. This was the part I liked best.

'Imagine my feelings,' the princess said. 'I had saved the life of the very man whose offer of marriage I had determined to reject, and whom I had steeled myself to detest, and with whom I was now thoroughly and hopelessly in love!'

I smiled and drew her down upon me, and sought her lips.

Old women began to appear around my wife, and her younger attendants dropped away. Even the pretty deaf-mute was banished, although I saw her sometimes about the palace, and I always took the opportunity to give her a friendly smile, at which she invariably held my eyes for just an instant before dropping her gaze with an almost imperceptible twitch of her full, moist lips.

After three months the old women advised me to sleep in my own bedchamber. Their advice, I soon learned, was in fact an edict. The old women ruled the realm of childbearing into which my wife was slipping slowly from my embrace, and were not to be disobeyed. They did not banish me entirely from her bed, and they acknowledged that a judicious amount of what they called conjugal exercise would benefit the health of both my wife and the child growing inside her, for the time being.

Of my own health, or my wishes, or any other trifling concern to do with me, nothing was said.

*

High summer found me listless and ill-tempered.

It was as if the murky water that filled my dreams now began to dampen my waking hours, obscuring everything in soft, clinging mist.

One morning, emerging from my wife's bedchamber, I encountered Doctor Bowl, who was waiting to enter the room. He had begun to examine my wife with increasing frequency, although he assured me there was no cause for concern, and that all was as it should be.

I liked the old man, who was remarkably hale for his age, and whose wits were as sharp as his features, the sight of which always put me in mind of dried berries and flint. As well as being a skilled physician he was a natural philosopher of great renown, and his eyes seemed to fathom secrets and wonders.

On a sudden impulse I asked if I might visit him, and receive some instruction from him in matters of which I felt myself sorely ignorant.

He gazed at me keenly – but not unkindly – and said he would be pleased to offer me whatever I might find of value from the storehouse of his learning.

I hastened to tell him my ambitions were modest, and I simply wished for a rudimentary understanding of the laws of nature, and the minds of men, and the workings of the animal kingdom.

He chuckled, and told me such an education could easily fill several lifetimes. When he saw I was crestfallen he smiled, and inclined his head, and said he found my intention highly praiseworthy, and my proposal would be an admirable way to employ my time in these summer months, when my wife was increasingly preoccupied with her pregnancy, and the court was quiet.

We made an appointment for the next day, and I thanked him.

All proceeded well for two months. Dr Bowl took my measure, and instructed me accordingly. I don't imply that he spared me hard work, only that he was a patient teacher who knew his pupil's limits.

For my part, I relished my studies. I felt my knowledge of the world becoming both deeper and more subtle. I acquired a grounding in moral philosophy, logic, rhetoric, grammar, and botany. I observed the stars, and learned their names, their influences, and the scheme of their movements through the sky. I felt as if my faculties, long unused, were growing in strength. I had hopes – which I kept to myself – that my powers of recollection would improve, and I would be able to lift the veil that lay over my past, and know more of my life before I came to the court.

One morning Dr Bowl told me the time had come for me to begin my study of the animal kingdom.

'I have prepared a demonstration for you,' he said.

He drew aside a curtain, opened a concealed door, and led me along a passageway to a chamber at the end of it.

I saw wooden benches, instruments, devices, bottles. Pale, fleshy objects suspended in fluids, misshapen by the distorting qualities of the glass behind which they floated, or perhaps misshapen in themselves.

Doctor Bowl approached a bench. A flat dish lay upon it, and there was something in the dish.

'Here,' he said, 'I have exposed the nervous system so that you may observe how the muscles may be stimulated.'

I saw what was in the dish.

It was a frog, flayed to reveal the inside of the body, and all its organs.

Then, as I stood rooted to the spot, I saw the eyes moving.

The creature was alive. My legs began to shake. The frog's eyes seemed to seek mine, and to gaze at me imploringly. My head became light, and I staggered.

Doctor Bowl glanced at me sharply. 'Are you unwell?'

I made no reply.

'If you feel you must vomit,' the doctor continued, 'have the goodness to use the basin that is beneath the bench behind you.'

I turned and fled.

I remained alone in my rooms for two days, after which, in answer to repeated messages, I went to the princess in her bedchamber.

Even though it was but a matter of days since I'd visited her – and lain with her, coupling carefully and tenderly – the sight of her took me aback. Her belly was swollen, her breasts heavy, and her features inflamed.

She bid me lie down beside her, but did not draw back the bedcovers. She stroked my cheek, and took my hand.

With a smile she said we must forgo our accustomed intimacy for a time. She expected to be delivered of our child within the month, and the crones who attended her had decreed that I should not appear in her presence until that time.

As my wife placed my hand gently upon her belly I forced myself to smile at her, and stifled my impulse to recoil. I told her I would pass every moment of our separation yearning for her touch.

I began to be assailed by a fear of what would emerge from my wife's womb.

I lay awake at night in torment. If I succeeded in sleeping at all I was haunted by visions of unnatural creatures, deformed and monstrous. As the days and nights passed my terror only grew, and I dreaded what our chid might be.

One evening as I paced through the palace, lost in thought and blind to my surroundings, I found myself face to face with the pretty young lady-in-waiting. This time she did not lower her gaze when our eyes met.

I followed her to a flight of narrow stone steps in a part of the palace unknown to me. We began to ascend the steps. She glanced over her shoulder at me and smiled, and we quickened our pace.

Later, when we had slaked our lust, I gazed up at the bare ceiling of her meagre chamber, and began to speak. She lay on her side, watching my face.

I felt a great compulsion to unburden myself, secure in the knowledge that she heard nothing of what I said. My thoughts and fears gushed from me as if a cork were drawn from a bottle in which noxious liquid has been long fermenting. I spoke of the visions of deformity that plagued me, and of my fears that my wife would give birth to a monster. I confessed my horror that my own seed was tainted by a secret in my past, which was concealed from me by an evil enchantment under which I had fallen.

I spoke in this way until I had emptied myself of all my terrors. I saw that my companion was asleep, lying on her back with her eyes closed, a tranquil smile upon her lips. I rose from her bed and made my way back to my own chambers.

The next morning I heard my wife cry out. I sprang from my bed, and by the time I had dressed myself a servant was at my door, waiting to take me to her.

I found her clasping a swaddled child to her breast. She gazed at me with wide, exhausted eyes. The ghost of a smile appeared on her lips, very slowly. She seemed a great distance away.

'My prince,' she said, 'you have a son.'

Before I knew it one of her attendants had taken the little bundle from her and was approaching me, simpering and holding it out to me. As if in a dream I took it from her. I looked down at the face. It was smooth and pink. The eyes opened and I saw they were blue. The infant gazed up at me gravely, as if it looked clear into my soul, and judged me for what was there.

My sight became clouded. I felt the child begin to slip from my grasp.

I heard cries of terror, and glimpsed swift movements as darkness descended upon me, and enclosed me.

*

When the light returned I was here, in my new quarters.

Lord Abel was with me. He attended to me solicitously, and satisfied himself as to my recovery. Then he left me, saying he would return shortly.

My chamber was well-appointed. The windows offered a magnificent prospect. I gazed down, from a great height, upon the palace grounds, and the distant forest, and beyond it, on the far horizon, the hazy mountains. I was prevented from seeing what was directly below me by the bars on the windows.

I inspected everything that had been provided for me, and explored every aspect of my new home, until I found myself standing before the heavy oaken door. Slowly I reached out and tested the handle, knowing what I would discover.

Some time later I heard a key turn in the lock, and Lord Abel entered, securing the door behind him. He bid me be seated, and took a chair opposite me, studying my features. Finally he leaned back, and in a gentle voice he told me what he required me to know.

I was ailing, he told me, and my wits were somewhat disordered. My son, however, was well, and had been saved from being dashed to the floor by the prompt action of a serving-woman who, with great alacrity, had thrown herself to the ground and caught the child at the moment I flung him from me.

'Wait!' I cried, 'Surely I did not fling him from me! Was I not seized by a fainting fit, and did not the infant slip from my hands?'

Lord Abel shook his head with a sad smile. 'No doubt, sire, that is how it seems to you. But all who were present saw what you did. I was there myself, although perhaps you failed to notice me. After you were taken away, I questioned every witness, and coaxed them to give an honest account of what they saw, even though some were reluctant to indict you at first. But finally every testimony was in agreement. You flung the child from you.'

'But my wife,' I said, 'would never think such a thing of me. I beg you, tell me she believes I meant no harm to the little creature.'

Lord Abel raised an eyebrow. 'An interesting choice of words,' he murmured, then he leaned forward and adopted a confidential tone:

'The feelings of the princess, sire, were thrown further into turmoil, immediately after your violent treatment of the child, by learning of the manner and the company in which you had passed the previous evening.'

I regarded him dumbly. He drew his chair nearer to mine.

My wife, he told me, knew of my infidelity. He made no attempt to conceal the fact that he himself had informed her of my transgression.

The pretty young lady-in-waiting, far from being unable to hear and speak, heard everything, and spoke of all she saw to Lord Abel. She had been placed in our household by him, to be his eyes and ears from the first day of our marriage.

Thus he was aware not only of my fornication with the girl, but of all I said that evening as I poured out the fears and horrors that wracked me.

I asked him when I might be permitted to see my wife and son.

'The princess believes,' he said, 'that after you have recovered your wits sufficiently to be truly penitent, a time may come when you might be reunited with her. Until then, however, she has been persuaded of the inadvisability of enjoying your company, and of you being permitted to see the child.'

'And will such a time come, Lord Abel?'

He pursed his lips. 'I think not, sire.'

'Will you not reconsider, if I promise to be good?'

'I will be plain,' he said. 'You have served your purpose. We shall find another husband for the princess.'

'No! Do not tell me that!'

'Are you certain,' Abel said softly, 'that you would wish it otherwise? Will you not confess that the thought of laying with your wife now fills you with disgust, and that you believe yourself to be, in some fashion… inhuman?'

'As result of sorcery!' I cried. 'I have fallen under an enchantment! The princess found me, and it was… I was…'

'You were what, prince Anton?'

I tried to clear my head, but it was in vain.

Lord Abel rose from his chair. He paused at the door with the heavy key in his hand and inquired if there was anything further I wanted for my comfort.

I asked him to bring me some flies.

All this is a dream, of course.

When I awake, at night, I glory in my true nature. I feel the water swirling around me, and press myself against the bodies of my kind. We copulate ceaselessly, and I yearn to see the world filled with beautiful, shimmering spawn.

Loss Adjustment

'Don't let anybody tell you how you should grieve,' Lisa said to Robin, and continued telling him how he should grieve.

'It's important,' she said, 'not to deny your vulnerability. Bereavement can be a kind of gift, and it can actually offer a wonderful opportunity for personal growth.'

Lisa had gained some type of qualification in counselling shortly before Cassie died, although Robin had only a sketchy idea of how she'd acquired it, and what she was now qualified to do. She'd talked about it at some length, but he hadn't really been listening. Still, she'd been generous with her advice since Cassie's death, and this was the third time she'd come to the flat in as many weeks. On the first two occasions she'd shown up with food she'd made for him, but this time she just brought a bottle of wine. Robin still wasn't used to seeing her without David, his old college friend, who'd started dating Lisa just a few weeks after Robin moved in with Cassie. The two couples quickly became close, and as Robin turned thirty he'd found himself slipping into a life defined by all the things they did together: dinners, movies, gigs, drugs, festivals.

Then, six months ago, David and Lisa broke up. It was acrimonious, and when it was over Lisa seemed to have been awarded custody of their friends. She began spending more time with Cassie, but Robin no longer saw much of David, and if he wanted to hang out with him he was forced to make arrangements that felt surreptitious and shameful. On the increasingly rare occasions when they met, David talked incessantly about Lisa, extracting information from Robin about what she was doing, and trying to make him agree she was a bitch. Robin gradually stopped making an effort to see him.

When Cassie was killed David didn't get in touch, and he failed to respond to Robin's texts about the funeral. He'd made no contact since then.

Lisa, however, was another matter. Here she was again, and Robin wasn't sure if he was supposed to sleep with her. It was too soon, surely? Only a month since he'd lost Cassie.

That was the expression people used — that he'd lost her — but he wasn't comfortable with it. He didn't like the implication that he'd somehow mislaid her, and she might turn up again at some point.

As it happened, he'd had a few dreams since her death in which something like that seemed to happen. In the dreams he was alone in the flat, having realised that it contained a room he'd never previously noticed. Before he could explore it Cassie came home unexpectedly. She'd been away on a modelling assignment in an unspecified foreign country, and she seemed angry about something, and refused to meet his eye. When Robin tried to show her the hidden room he was unable to find it. She became scornful, and Robin felt a growing sense of panic. Then, in the dream, he began to cry. At this point he invariably woke up, and found himself to be dry-eyed. As the dream faded, and he observed that Cassie's side of the bed was empty, he was assailed by none of the sudden anguish or aching loneliness that other people claimed to have experienced in similar circumstances. Robin wondered if there was something wrong with him.

Now Lisa was talking about Rumi, and the poet's contention that grief was a garden of compassion.

Robin nodded and tried to look thoughtful. He had no problem with this stuff, and he endorsed its sentiments wholeheartedly, and found it interesting, but none of it mattered. It made no difference to what went through his mind while he listened politely to people telling him how terrible it must be for him.

And it was terrible, he knew, but sometimes he wondered if all those people would have been quite as horrified and despondent as they professed themselves to be if Cassie hadn't been so staggeringly beautiful. The fact of her beauty, combined with the stupidity of her death in a hit-and-run accident, seemed to provoke feelings in many people – some of them strangers to Robin – which they expressed with a ferocity that often took him aback.

Thank god he and Cassie didn't have children. The absence of this extra garnish of tragedy had spared him, he thought, from a level of sympathy and outrage he would have found overwhelming.

Nonetheless, Robin sometimes fantasised about what would have happened if he'd been left to bring up a child alone. Preferably an adorable little girl. She would be three, or perhaps four. Old enough to understand, in her innocent way, that her mummy wasn't coming home, but young enough for her tender, yearning heart to propel her frequently into his arms, especially in public. He would be a soulful, brooding figure, who could be persuaded to smile and laugh only by his little girl. Women would find him irresistible, aroused by his refusal to countenance another relationship, and eager to provide whatever small comfort they could, in the form of unconditional sex. When they saw him leading his daughter by the hand into the park, or placing her gently on his lap in a coffee shop, his devotion to her shining through the deep, mysterious shadow cast around him by his grief, they would wet themselves.

Whoa, Robin thought, dial it back.

These fantasies, which usually began with what he was sure were authentic feelings of pathos, always ended up going too far.

'It was so extraordinary,' Lisa was saying, 'seeing the whirling dervishes there in a church in Hoxton.'

Wait, Robin thought, what? He'd spaced out for a couple of minutes there, and what Lisa was now saying sounded weird. He widened his eyes, indicating his interest and surprise.

'It's an amazing place,' Lisa said, 'and it does a lot of multi-faith work. The priest who runs it – or is it a vicar? I'm not sure – anyway, he's got such a cool attitude about other religions, and he makes everyone so welcome, even if you don't believe anything at all. Really inspirational vibe. He's a lovely man.'

'Sounds great,' Robin said.

'What a lot of people don't realise is that Rumi was actually a Sufi holy man as well as a poet, and when he writes about the beloved, he means God, and so when he talked about being reunited with his beloved he meant dying, and that's why they don't mourn his death. It's a celebration for them.'

'Right. For who?'

'The dervishes.'

'Right, right. And that's why they whirl, is it?'

'That,' Lisa said, 'and other reasons.'

'Maybe I should try it. Give it a whirl, know what I mean?'

Lisa smiled, but Robin had the impression she didn't get the joke. Or maybe she did, but she didn't think it was appropriate, because she was trying to help him heal, or grow, or whatever, and he was showing insufficient gratitude by being flippant. Perhaps she felt he was mocking her sincerity, or patronising her.

She topped up their drinks.

Robin raised his glass. 'Cheers,' he said, and drank, enjoying the feeling of the wine in his throat. It tasted expensive.

When he put his glass down he saw that Lisa was gazing at him across the table, her chin resting on her hands. He waited for her to say something.

She sighed. 'It's so strange, isn't it?'

'I suppose so.'

'Look,' she said, 'I hope this doesn't sound creepy, but would you mind if I took something of hers?'

'What do you mean?'

'Something to remember her by.'

'Oh, I see. I suppose so. I mean, yes, that's fine. But she didn't have very many things. Ornaments, or pictures, or things like that.'

'No, nothing big,' Lisa said. 'I just meant clothes.'

'Which clothes?'

'Just something she wore. Nothing important. Unless you've made arrangements for everything. Have you?'

'No, I was waiting for Ed to get back. Her brother.'

'Where's he gone? I thought he was back.'

'No, he just came back for the funeral. Then he left again straight away, because his contract in Latvia only had six weeks to run. Two weeks now.'

'Estonia.'

'Oh right, Estonia. I always get them mixed up. Anyway, he said he'd help me sort everything out when he gets back. You know, various arrangements.'

Robin reached for the wine bottle and refilled his glass, and remembered to pour some for Lisa. He picked up his glass, but put it down again without drinking from it. He spread his fingers and ran his hand along the grain of the wooden kitchen table. Arrangements. He was glad he could leave them, whatever they might turn out to be, until Ed got back.

Lisa was looking at him expectantly.

'Take whatever you want,' Robin said, 'in the way of clothes. Go ahead.'

'Thanks. It was just those leggings, really. You know, the sports leggings with the zebra stripe?'

'I'm not sure.'

'I'll get them and show you, shall I?'

'Okay.'

Lisa stood up and walked towards the bedroom. Robin vaguely remembered Cassie wearing some striped leggings when she and Lisa went running in the park. He drank his wine.

After five minutes Robin went to see what Lisa was doing.

He paused in the bedroom doorway. The zebra print leggings were on the bed and Lisa was standing in front of the dressing table. For an instant Robin thought Lisa was looking at herself in the mirror but then he saw she was holding something in front of her face. She was shaking, and breathing deeply, as if she were trying to inhale what was in her hands. She looked up and saw his reflection in the mirror. Her eyes were red.

'Sorry,' she said.

Robin saw she was holding one of Cassie's brassieres.

'Sorry,' Lisa repeated. She rubbed her eyes with the back of her hand.

'It's all right,' Robin said, 'you can take that if you like.'

Lisa nodded. 'Thanks. We were the same size. You probably knew.'

'No, I… right. It's fine.'

'Thanks. I'll take it instead,' Lisa said. She shot him a sudden anxious glance in the mirror. 'It wasn't one you bought for her, was it? Part of a set, or something?'

'No,' Robin said, 'I never bought that kind of stuff for her.'

'I'll just go and wash my face, if that's okay.'

'Of course.'

As Robin went back to the kitchen he remembered how he'd been on the point of buying lingerie for Cassie, not long after they met, but then he read something online about how much women disliked being given underwear, and expected to display themselves in it. It made Robin think – really think – and he considered it a formative moment, to which he was always grateful whenever he recalled how close he'd come to behaving like a particular type of prick.

*

Lisa tipped the last of the wine into their glasses. Her open bag was beside her on the table, and Cassie's bra was trailing out. She saw Robin glancing at it and stuffed it further down into the bag.

When she looked up she held Robin's gaze. Her lip began to tremble and her eyes filled with tears.

'I'm sorry,' she whispered, almost choking, and then her face collapsed and she began to wail, shuddering and sobbing helplessly.

Robin reached over the table to take her hand, but Lisa didn't seem to notice, and he thought better of it, and picked up his glass instead.

After a minute or so the flow of Lisa's tears subsided. She dabbed at her eyes with some tissues from her bag, and blew her nose.

'Oh god,' she said, 'you must think I'm an idiot.'

'Of course not. Don't say that. We all loved her.'

'I know,' Lisa said, starting to cry again, 'but I was in love with her.'

'Well, yes,' Robin said, 'we were all in love with her, weren't we?'

Lisa paused, with the crumpled tissues halfway to her eyes. 'So you knew about David?'

'What about David?'

'Oh god! I'm sorry! I thought you meant…'

'No, what am I supposed to know?'

'Oh god.'

'Fuck. Are you saying they had an affair?'

'No!' Lisa shook her head fiercely. 'No they bloody didn't!'

'What do you mean, then?'

Lisa pressed her lips together, as if to prevent herself speaking, and looked down at her hands, breathing heavily through her nose. She seemed to be making an effort to compose herself. Finally she looked up at Robin. She reached over the table and grasped his hand, in decisive contrast to his earlier, tentative attempt to take hers.

'Look,' she said, giving his hand a little shake, 'I didn't let it happen.'

'You mean he tried to?'

'He wanted to. He was obsessed with her. But I stopped him. That's why we broke up. Didn't you know?'

'No. I had no idea. Shit. But what about Cassie? Did she know? I mean, what did she think? Did she want to… you know…?'

'I don't know!' Lisa let go of his hand and looked away.

'I don't understand,' Robin said. 'If that was the reason why you and David broke up, because he wanted to fuck Cassie, then surely she must have known. Didn't she? I mean, why didn't you tell her?'

Lisa turned to face him again. She was pale. 'I couldn't,' she said. 'I couldn't talk to her about it. I couldn't bear to.'

'Why not?'

'Because I wanted her myself. In the same way. Don't you see?'

'Oh god.'

'I'm sorry. What a mess.'

Mess? Robin thought it was a strange word to use about what had happened, as though they'd all been careless or sloppy about something they could have done better. But it wasn't a mess. It was horribly orderly. Ever since the moment he'd been informed of Cassie's death he'd experienced everything, including his memories, with great precision. Even his most inappropriate thoughts and feelings – especially those – had been oddly distinct, presenting themselves in high definition, with startling clarity. That was part of the problem.

Lisa was gazing at him sadly. 'Shall I go?' she said.

'Okay.'

Robin didn't move for a long time. He didn't know how long. His mind was empty except for the sound of the front door closing behind Lisa.

He stood up. He needed to move, to do something, go somewhere. He had to get out. He strode to the front door and opened it. But he didn't leave. He stood in the doorway, gazing at the familiar hallway, wondering why it hadn't changed.

What was he doing? There was nowhere he wanted to go. The thought of seeing people disgusted him. He slammed the door and walked back into the kitchen, but he didn't want to be there either. He went into the living room, then the bathroom, then back to the kitchen. Something was building inside him, some kind of pressure he couldn't escape from.

He picked up the chair Lisa had been sitting on and raised it above his head and brought it down onto the table as hard as he could. One of the wooden struts between the chair's legs splintered and the wine bottle rolled off the table and smashed on the floor. Robin threw the chair at the wall, and it broke a picture.

It was their fault. All of them. Not just the driver, the stupid, drunken prick behind the wheel of the stolen car, who still hadn't been found, but was probably just a kid, some pathetic kid, it was Lisa too, and David, and the creepy fuckers who hugged him, and looked sad – they'd all tried to take her away from him.

Now he understood what David had really wanted from him when he kept asking him about Lisa after the break-up. He was trying to reach through Robin as if he were a phantom, and to reach through Lisa, and touch Cassie.

And every time Lisa had gone running with Cassie, moving and sweating and laughing in rhythm with her, she was trying to run away with her, and have her for herself.

They'd all been trying to take her, and then death came for her, and showed them how it was done.

He walked into the bedroom. The striped leggings were still on the bed where Lisa had left them. He stared at them. Why hadn't he known? Even Cassie had done it: she had taken herself away from him.

She had left him. They had all robbed him, and he hated them, all of them.

He picked up the leggings and tried to tear them apart, but the elasticated material was too dense and strong, and wouldn't give. He pulled and stretched them with all his might, screaming at them, not words, just noises, trying to destroy them, but he couldn't. He raised them to his face and starting biting and chewing at the fabric, trying to gnaw a hole that would let him get his fingers into the fibres and rip the garment to pieces.

Then it hit him. The scent she used. And beneath that, very faintly, her own smell. The private aroma of her body.

He staggered, and caught sight of himself in the mirror. He looked like Lisa, holding Cassie's clothing to his face and breathing in her smell.

He roared at his reflection, flecking the mirror with spittle. He felt a howl of rage and misery rising up though his body, then tearing at his throat as he let it out and heard its terrible, animal sound.

He flung the leggings from him and sank to his knees beside the bed, and leaned against it as if he were a child at evening prayers. He sobbed, clawing at the bedcovers and wrapping them around himself like a shroud. Slowly he heaved himself up and rolled onto the bed.

A small part of him continued to observe what was happening, and to comment on it. So, it said, this is what it's like. This is the feeling.

But after a few moments that voice was silent.

Robin greeted the sorrow that had been waiting for him so patiently, and allowed it to possess him.

Prank versus Dick Move

The Tao of Prank and the Singularity of the Dick Move: a Discourse.

Dr Andrew Wemmell PhD, lecturer in social psychology, London University.

Premises

a) A prank is understood to require an object, or victim: the prankee.

b) The dick move may be foolish or deplorable without impinging on others.

c) This paper proposes the practice of pranking as a Tao, or 'way', in contrast to the dick move as a discrete act, and poses the question: "Prank or Dick Move?"

You order a pizza to the address of a cemetery. When the delivery arrives you're waiting at the gates, dressed in tattered, muddy clothing. You offer to pay with a ten shilling note.

Prank? Certainly. Dick move? Possibly, if there is malice towards the prankee. But if the malicious intent is justified as retaliation for a perceived offence on the part of the pizza delivery guy, who previously acted like a dick, this is not necessarily a dick move.

Before going out to a dinner party, tell the new babysitter the twins are asleep, and ask her to check on them in an hour. However, you have only one child.

A prank. But if, for the amusement of your fellow diners, you put your phone on speaker to take the babysitter's terrified call, it partakes of a dick move. Further, if you then justify your behaviour to your wife on the way home by claiming the babysitter had it coming, this would indicate a shift to total dick move, and that you're drunk, you dick.

If you stand outside a dry cleaner's in your underwear, angrily checking your watch, they'll eventually pay you to go away.

Research suggest the most likely outcome of this experiment is, in fact, that the store manager threatens to call the police.

However, let us postulate a hypothetical prankster – we'll call him Tristram – and examine how he might deflect the manager's hostility by initiating a secondary prank. For example, if Tristram has a glib, persuasive manner – what some people might call charm or charisma – he may convince the manager he is performing a 'stunt' of the type staged by students to raise money for charity. Tristram's manner is so persuasive that after a few minutes the manager donates money to the supposed charity on whose behalf Tristram is staging the alleged stunt, thereby providing Tristram with funds to visit the pub, where he gloats over his achievement to a friend – let's call him Andrew.

Furthermore, when the prankster – in this instance, Tristram – has a facility for improvisation, and is utterly shameless, he may be tempted to escalate these actions. Hence the premise of the prank as Tao: a way of being. This praxis may create a cycle of anticipation and gratification, leading Tristram to lose sight of the distinction between a prank and a dick move, until he himself becomes a total, insufferable dick.

Other factors may influence such behaviour if Tristram, as a university student, encounters ideas of moral philosophy he is unequipped to understand. When he attends a lecture on Nietzsche in the company of Andrew, his (then) friend, Tristram fails to see the nuance in Nietzsche's thinking. But later, in the pub, two attractive female undergraduates find Tristram's facile regurgitation of misunderstood Nietzschean ideas (and Tristram himself) more compelling than Andrew's exegesis, and Andrew as a person.

Tristram's introduction to Nietzsche marks a shift in his conception of the prank, and its praxis. Until this point, Tristram's efforts have been relatively harmless, evidenced by the willingness of Andrew – whose ethical standards are clearly higher – to participate in some of them. For example:

Annoying neighbour? Leave a note on their car: "Sorry about the scratch, but I've patched it up so you can hardly see it."

In this instance any detrimental impact on the prankee is justified by the fact that Tristram and Andrew – sharing lodgings at this time – consider the neighbour's behaviour obnoxious, particularly his repeated complaints about the volume of the music they play.

Travelling by Eurostar, wait until the train is beneath the Channel, then emerge from a toilet cubicle apparently unaware of the fish flapping from your pocket.

This may be construed as a victimless prank. It passes largely unnoticed, or is ignored by the few passengers who witness it. However, the video clip goes viral.

The prank was conceived by Andrew, and the video was filmed and edited by him. However, it features Tristram as the onscreen actor, and has the effect of enhancing his social media profile, and the impression of an irrepressibly playful nature. The reality is very different. But most people, particularly women, seem unable to penetrate what appears to be a boyish sense of mischief, and see the cruelty beneath it.

For a case in point, let us return to the pizza-based prank mentioned earlier. It is conceived by Tristram and Andrew as an act of revenge on the pizza delivery guy. This individual became hostile when Tristram, alleging a pizza was delivered late, attempted to negotiate a discount, using increasingly absurd arguments about time, space, and the nature of reality. The pizza guy threatened violence, and was paid in full.

Tristram and Andrew then speculate about pranking the delivery guy with the cemetery idea. But Tristram decides it's too much hassle. Andrew believes this is the end of the matter. Far from it. Tristram is still determined to take revenge. Over the next two weeks, he tracks down the delivery guy and repeatedly vandalises his motor scooter, causing him eventually to lose his job.

It is now that Andrew sees the darker side of Tristram's nature. What makes the discovery especially disturbing for him is the failure of others in their social circle to share his insight. Andrew's then girlfriend, Anna, expresses admiration for Tristram's resolve and commitment in taking his revenge, which she considers justified.

Go into a shoe store. Surreptitiously insert a note into the largest shoe you can find: "This used to be my home, you heartless bastard. Signed, Old Woman."

The above is one of the 'victimless' pranks that Andrew devises at this period, in an attempt to reconnect with what he sees as the essentially ludic, harmless nature of pranking. However, Tristram is losing interest in pranks that fail to humiliate or wound a victim. He insists a prankster must be present when the prank is executed, and must confront the victim, who must understand that he or she has been pranked, and by whom.

Inform a close friend that you will give his fiancée – let's call her Anna – a ride to Scotland, to visit her parents, at the start of the summer vacation, when the friend stays on at the university to complete his dissertation. Reassure your friend that Anna will be safe from any sexual overtures on your part, as your own girlfriend will also be in the car. However, this is untrue. You seduce Anna, and spend the next ten days with her.

This is unequivocally a dick move, despite the perpetrator telling the friend (Andrew) he should see the funny side, particularly as his dissertation is titled *Romantic Love as a Tool of Cultural Capital in Emerging Post-Colonial Societies*. The friend, however, is devastated, especially when

Anna breaks off their engagement.

Wait until a friend is experiencing stress as a result of a failed personal relationship and his dissertation being rejected, then alienate him from everyone in his social circle by claiming he has had a psychotic breakdown. When the friend accuses you of plotting against him, tell everyone his accusations prove that he is suffering from paranoia.

Here we pass beyond the matrix of prank-or-dick-move, and perceive the perpetrator's duplicitous sociopathy. The duplicity is compounded by his insistence that he is motivated only by concern for the victim. Ironically, the frustration the victim experiences in his efforts to expose his tormentor exacerbates his mental and emotional fragility to the extent that he is hospitalised briefly.

Make repeated assurances to a friend that you are committed to a future in academia, like him, before leaving the university for a career in advertising. Eight years later, the friend learns that you are using prank ideas originally devised wholly, or in part, by him, for the purposes of 'native advertising' on behalf of various brands. The Eurostar/fish prank is replicated, and the pizza/cemetery stunt is staged, and is so successful that it becomes a meme, which the friend sees practically every fucking time he goes online.

Nobody can escape their karma for ever.

*

You decide to teach an old friend – let's call him Tristram – a lesson. With some diligent research, and a little light hacking, you discover that he conducts extramarital affairs, and is a member of online 'dating' sites for married people.

Meanwhile, you establish that your one-time fiancée, Anna, is now living in Australia, and has no contact with Tristram or anyone in his circle, or any proximity to his social media connections. You construct an online identity for 'Anna', using information you hold about her, and photographs you've kept. In the guise of 'Anna' you subscribe to the dating site, and contact Tristram, saying you've discovered him on the site, and you live close to him! You confess you still think about the fling you had on your trip to Scotland, and you want to rekindle that passion. Naturally, Tristram responds. He is vain, lustful and stupid, and you (Andrew) expected nothing less. You ('Anna') set up an assignation at a bar, where you (Andrew) will confront Tristram and reveal that you are 'Anna'. The rest is a surprise. What a terrific prank!

*

I expected him to be angry, and he was, although he concealed it quite well.

He hadn't changed in looks or manner. Typically, he noted that my own appearance had deteriorated since we last saw each other, and that my hair was thinner and my paunch larger. He also remarked upon my lack of professional success, suggesting I was living in the basement of my mother's house and spending all my time online, when he knew perfectly well my mother died several years ago (although it's true that I live in her house, and it does have a basement). I could see he bitterly resented the exemplary prank I'd played on him, although, naturally, he denied it was exemplary and said it lacked the creativity of a true prank.

When I accused him of having stolen ideas of mine, and profited from them, he laughed in my face. His attitude was predictable in another respect too. He'd always been stingy, and, despite his anger, he allowed me to buy him a drink, asking for a cocktail, and noting with satisfaction that it was expensive.

He finished the drink quickly and left. I followed him at a discreet distance, and watched him get into his big SUV. When he drove out of the car park I tailed him – with some difficulty – in my small car. As I'd calculated, the drug began to take effect after about ten minutes. He pulled into the side of the road. By the time I'd parked behind him and walked to his vehicle he was slumped over the wheel.

A man wakes up in a locked room. At regular intervals, a hatch opens and food appears. Eventually the man abandons any attempt to escape, or to bargain with his captor, or to threaten him. He realises that he won't be found or rescued. He told nobody about the assignation he was attending, because of its clandestine – and shameful – nature. He is a victim of his own guilty conscience. After two years he begins to go mad.

There you have it: a perfect prank. Any imputation of a dick move is baseless: the victim deserves his fate. Deliciously, the prank conforms to Tristram's own precepts: the prankster confronts his victim, who knows he is being pranked, and by whom.

And so it begins: the Way of the Prank – the Tao. There is one prank, and one victim. The prank continues. Something I learned from

Tristram is that you must see the prank through until the end. And I shall.

The Glade

I found the manuscript on a visit to Aberdeen, when a sky as grey as the city beneath it prompted me to shelter in a junk shop from the threat of rain. I'd been wandering aimlessly to kill a couple of hours before leaving for the airport, but my bags were packed at the hotel, and I didn't want to get soaked.

I enjoy browsing in junk shops, although they usually turn out to be less promising than they look. You peer in through a grimy window at a disarray that's artfully contrived to make you wonder if it conceals a mislaid Rembrandt, or at least some Clarice Cliff china. A few minutes inside the shop is enough to remind you that everything is there because it was thrown out by someone. This place was no different, and I saw nothing that interested me. I wasn't looking very hard. My mind was elsewhere, thinking about my late wife. It was a year since her death, and I was in Aberdeen to tie up some business affairs with her family. Now everything was settled, and I couldn't help feeling that my final tie with her was severed. It was a sombre day in more ways than one.

But the rain didn't arrive, and I was on my way out of the shop when I passed a table with two wicker baskets on it. One was full of children's annuals from the 1970s, and the other contained a few bibles that appeared to have been chucked into it from across the room. I've always liked looking at old bibles. Often they've been passed down through several generations, and sometimes people write interesting

126

things inside them. Once I found a bible in which someone had filled the margins of every page with hair-raising blasphemy, made all the more disturbing by the meticulous neatness of the handwriting.

The bibles in the wicker basket didn't seem particularly special. One had a label inside the front cover, announcing that it had been awarded as a prize in scripture class to Elizabeth McCracken in 1913, and another featured a few colour plates that some people might have found amusing as a type of kitsch.

The next one I picked up appeared nondescript, but something about it made me pause as I was about to replace it. The back cover didn't quite close properly. It seemed oddly bulky. Closer inspection revealed an envelope, which had been sandwiched inside the book for so long it had become stuck to the back cover as firmly as if it were glued in place. The envelope itself was sealed. I made a surreptitious attempt to prise open the flap at the top, but it wouldn't budge.

I didn't want the man behind the desk at the back of the shop to notice my interest, so I put the bible back and inspected a nearby bookshelf dedicated to Hobbies and Pastimes. After a moment I selected a book on the history of Scottish steam trains. Then, as if struck by an afterthought, I went back for the bible.

Arranging my features into what I hoped was a guileless expression, I approached the desk. The man held out his hand for the books, flipped them open briefly, and handed them back.

'Twenty pounds,' he said.

I smiled at him. 'Would you take fifteen?'

'I would not.'

I nodded and gave him twenty pounds.

I postponed further investigation of the envelope until I got back to London. I didn't want to unsettle fellow passengers on my flight by apparently trying to rip apart a bible. They might have got the wrong idea.

It was late evening before I settled at my desk with a whiskey, and set to work. I tried again to prise the envelope from the bible's back cover, but I couldn't unpeel it without the risk of damage. Eventually I steamed open the flap. What was inside appeared to be a manuscript, on several sheets of folded paper. They were packed extremely tightly, but finally I got them out and unfolded them carefully. The first sheet seemed to be the final page of a covering letter, the rest of which was missing. It was handwritten in ink, and read as follows:

and finally, I enclose a fair copy, in his own hand, of the document my great-uncle Pascoe discovered on his famous voyage. When I was a little boy I saw the original on several occasions, but I was never permitted to touch it, for it looked as though it might crumble to pieces at any moment. Indeed, it has probably now done so; even in those distant days of my childhood the coarse parchment was already yellowed with age, and the writing upon it was almost illegible in places, especially towards the end, when it appeared that the wretched author had made his own ink out of whatever was to hand.

I have no way of knowing whether other copies exist, so this may be the only one. I think you'll agree it makes interesting reading, although not, perhaps, for the faint-hearted. And not, of course, for the young, or the more impressionable of the womenfolk. I trust your discretion in this, as in all things.

128

I hope we shall see you in the summer.

Fondly, as ever,

George.

There was no date or other identifying information, which presumably would have appeared, if anywhere, on the first page of the letter.

The rest of the document was different. The paper was thicker, and of a slightly smaller size than the covering letter. It looked older. The same was true of the handwriting, which was clearly the work of someone other than the author of the letter, unless he'd taken a lot of trouble to create that impression. I reminded myself that this was a copy of an even older manuscript, and as I read it I found myself visualising that crumbling document, 'yellowed with age'.

The story begins with no preamble, simply a date. I won't say anything else about it. What follows is a faithful reproduction of the document.

*

June 4

I begin writing this journal with an unruly conflict in my heart. I have a powerful desire to preserve the details of my story for posterity, and perhaps this compulsion is shared by all those who find themselves in circumstances as unfortunate as my own. And yet the more truthfully I write, the less probable it is that I will be believed. In the unlikely event that anyone should stumble across this remote spot, and the unlikelier possibility of him chancing upon this document, he will surely surmise that these are the wild imaginings of a deranged sensibility. In my mind's eye I see the stranger fling these tattered sheets into the nearby undergrowth, with a scowl and an oath, before continuing whatever odd business should have brought him to this god-forsaken spot.

And yet I write, and as I sit at my makeshift table, clumsily forming the characters that have become so unfamiliar to me since last I committed words to paper, perhaps I begin to discern my true motive. Do I hope, by keeping this record, to dispel the shadow of madness which creeps over me? A thrill of terror shakes me as I write the word – madness – and I see it shrieking up at me from the page. Merely entertaining the idea is a stratagem of the mind to destroy itself, and here in my darkness, as the thick jungle soaks up the dying light, I find myself cursing the God who gave me a brain. Perhaps I am already committed to the Devil's hands. Three days ago I caught sight of my reflection in a stagnant pool, but I saw only a pair of burning eyes set into a bearded face which I did not recognise as my own. Today, on several occasions, I thought I heard my name being called: every sound from the forest, every creak or tick, every insectile chirrup, every stark animal cry – all seem to form syllables that hang in the air long after their source has faded.

I am becoming weary of this unaccustomed labour, and with the clumsy instrument that serves me for a pen. Now I must prepare for another night in which my fitful sleep will be haunted by yearning dreams.

June 5

With increasing frequency I find myself drifting through the day like flotsam upon a sea of time, with little awareness of what I do. My thoughts wander, disappear, and then become suddenly fixed, with startling intensity, on small details of my work or my surroundings. At times my inability to control my mental faculties fills me with dread. Am I destined to become a witless savage, aimlessly roaming the forest until I die?

Reading over what I wrote yesterday I begin to doubt the wisdom of keeping this chronicle. Where previously the substance of my despair was all confined within myself, and I could escape it on occasion, now I have provided myself with material evidence of it. I have tricked myself, like a crafty gaoler in charge of a drunken felon, into writing the confession that condemns me.

June 6

Today I killed a bird with my bow. It was ugly, though colourful, but the meat was as tender as any I have tasted.

June 7

Again today I seemed to hear my name being tossed among the treetops and whispered through the unquiet foliage. In the world I left behind, the mind would sometimes fix upon a popular melody until it drove one to distraction, and I now seem similarly obsessed with the sound of my own name.

See: a tear has fallen, and made the ink run. I am thinking about a particular song, and a certain person singing it, and I must stop.

June 8

I have explored the terrain around my camp to an extent of about five miles in every direction save due west, or as near due west as I can reckon. One reason for this omission is that I began my explorations to the south, and thence to the east and north, and I became so discouraged by the inhospitality of the terrain in every direction that I abandoned the task.

But In addition to this, I have a sense of foreboding about the land to my west. From the top of a tree beside my camp I can see a peak in that direction, perhaps twenty miles away: far beyond the range of an expedition I could make. Between myself and that solitary crest lies an unbroken vista of thick forest.

However, I awoke this morning with a strong determination to make a foray into that region. I suspect it was my sheer desperation to find a purpose for my distracted energies that drove me from my camp at sunrise with as many provisions as I could reasonably carry. But before I had travelled half a mile the sky darkened and torrential rain began to fall with such force I feared the entire forest was about to come crashing down around me. I made my way back, and here I sit, cold and miserable, as the deluge beats down outside my flimsy shelter as remorselessly as ever.

June 9.

The rain continues and I am a prisoner in my camp. The interruption of my plan seems to confirm my sense that the area I was attempting to explore is a place of mystery and tabu. Is the weather an omen of some kind? If so, I refuse to heed it, and it merely strengthens my purpose. I shall not be prevented!

I find myself laughing at my indignant resolve. But surely a man in my position, who feels the seeds of self-destruction plunging their roots into his soul, is permitted to rail a little in defiance of his destiny?

June 10.

I awoke to a clear sky, only to see that a part of the wooden stockade I have built around the shelter had been knocked down by a large branch in the night.

The repairs to the damage kept me occupied for most of the day. On several occasions I found myself gazing into the jungle, fascinated by the intricate play of light and shadow on the dense foliage, which seems to be woven into a gigantic pattern which I cannot properly discern because I am too close to it. Regarding my postponed expedition, I adamantly refuse to be deterred from undertaking it.

June 11.

Does any man suffer as I do, alone and uncertain, the plaything of a capricious fate? I am ashamed to lavish such pity on myself, and yet I feel I am sinking into a morass.

This morning I set out once again upon my expedition to the west. No thunderstorm erupted to impede my progress, and as I hacked my way through the undergrowth I felt a sense of elation. I had been labouring for perhaps three hours, and was certainly more than a mile from my shelter, when I observed that contrary to my expectation the foliage was becoming less dense. The canopy of trees overhead was as thick as ever but the vegetation beneath it was less impassable than any I had so far encountered at this distance from my camp. I covered another half a mile in a fairly short time, and had every intention of continuing further, when I stumbled into a small glade or clearing. It was almost uniformly circular in shape, and the flora around it appeared to be of lighter greens and gentler hues than that which prevails elsewhere.

I stood in the little glade, looking about me. Dappled sunlight played upon a carpet of soft, yielding moss. The air had a crispness most unusual for this moist and humid region, and there was a subtle fragrance in the atmosphere.

A feeling of great tranquillity overcame me. My troubles were lifted from my shoulders, as were the sorrows from my heart. I felt a loosening of indefinable bonds that constrained me, and I surrendered to freedom.

I seemed to flow out of myself, to escape my body, and to fill the little glade like a gas. I was sensible of every part of my surroundings: I could feel the ground beneath me, and at the same time I was brushed by the uppermost leaves of the trees. There were no thoughts in my mind, but neither was it empty. Rather, it was a comfortable refuge, in which I felt a sense of perfect harmony with all that was within me and outside me, until the distinction between the two dissolved entirely, and all was quiet joy.

I do not know for how long this sensation persisted. However, I was not unaware of time passing, as if I were in a trance; on the contrary, each facet of every moment was displayed to me with great clarity, and was infinitely full of itself, and of all possible moments.

There was a disturbance in the undergrowth at the edge of the glade, and I heard the cry of an animal. A subtle change took place. I recoiled from my abandoned state, and shuddered with dread as I saw a vision of what I might become if I should yield to the seductive tranquillity of that place. For in those moments of surrender was I not ceasing to be a man, and becoming an animal? A sensing, rather than a thinking creature?

Gathering my wits and my strength I turned and fled that place, and the yawning chasm of savagery into which I had so nearly tumbled. As I plunged through the jungle I knew that without my reasoning faculties, and the familiar thoughts which make me the person I can recognise as myself, I will become lost to the jungle around me, and indistinguishable from the padding, snarling beasts which inhabit it.

I reached the sanctuary of my camp, and now I am prostrated by fatigue.

June 12.
I did not stir from my camp all day.

June 13.

I had a strong desire to hunt this morning, although my supply of food is adequate. I set off from my shelter and roamed the edge of forest. I was presented with several opportunities for a kill, but did not take them. To be sure, making arrows is a tedious business, but some other force seemed to stay my hand on the occasions when prey – which is remarkably docile in this region – was within bowshot. I sought something, but I knew not what.

After two hours had passed in this way I sat down on a fallen tree trunk to rest. I had been there no longer than a minute when I heard a sound behind me. Carefully taking up my bow, I turned very slowly.

I found myself looking at a creature I was unable to identify. It was only a few feet away, but seemed oblivious to my presence. It made a sudden pecking motion, delving at the ground, and I saw it was a large bird, but of a species unlike any other I have seen. Its bearing was stately, and its plumage displayed a shimmering array of lovely colours. Its breast was of a red so rich as to be purple, which shaded by fine degrees along its body and wings, ending in a deep orange glow at the tip of its tail.

With as little movement as I could make, I fitted an arrow to my bow, raised it, and drew back the cord. As I was about to release the arrow the creature turned its head and its eyes met mine. Unblinking buttons of startling blue regarded me with utmost calmness. I felt sure it would take flight, and it raised itself up and spread its wings as if to do so, but instead of flying away it remained in that position, wings outstretched, body exposed.

I loosed the arrow. It struck home squarely in the breast of the creature, which continued to gaze at me. Slowly it drew in its wings, almost enfolding the shaft of the arrow, and dropped down dead.

On occasion in the past I have been troubled by sorrow and remorse after slaying a living creature but now I felt only a profound calm and wellbeing.

Pondering this on my way back to my camp it struck me that perhaps I have already become lost to my animal instincts. However, I knew my heart was neither callous nor savage. Instead I was exalted, as if by a kind of piety.

June 14.

When first I found myself divorced from the society of my fellows, I devised certain rules by which to regulate my conduct. One such stricture was that I should make use of any creature I slew, for food or other purposes. I could have obeyed my injunction simply by employing the feathers of the bird I killed yesterday in the manufacture of arrows, or perhaps extracting a little oil from its carcass. However, I determined to cook and eat the creature, as if I wished to honour it in some strange way.

But as I placed the first morsel of meat in my mouth I saw a vision of the animal's eyes just before it fell dead. The saliva drained from my jaws and my mouth became as dry as parchment. Nonetheless, I forced myself to consume every edible part of the bird, even though this was the work of an hour or more.

Had any person been present to observe me I must have made a sorry spectacle: a solitary Briton, in the depths of an unknown wilderness, devouring a meal he neither requires nor relishes, simply to satisfy an absurd notion of duty he has conceived in order to convince himself he remains a civilised being.

June 15 before dawn

I have awakened from a vivid dream. I saw an immense rock floating above the ground in a desert or wasteland. It was light and porous, like a decayed sponge. Despite *its size I was able to stretch my arms around it, and as I clasped it I felt myself sinking into it. I found myself looking down from a great height. I saw a man in a forest clearing. He was surrounded by an uncanny radiance that emanated from the trees and plants all around him. I began to fall, and as I fell I awoke.*

My limbs are heavy, and my mind is clouded. I will try to sleep again.

June 15, morning.

I awoke to an overcast day, but soon a fresh wind scattered the clouds, and the lethargy which had afflicted me. As my thoughts cleared it was as if a mist were dispelled, revealing the topic I have been concealing from myself. In an instant it became clear to me that I must revisit the little glade, and confront whatever awaits me. I will now set off without delay.

June 15, evening.

Words cannot convey my feelings nor adequately describe what has taken place. Would that the turmoil within me could flow out of my hand, and pass unimpeded through this clumsy pen, and burn itself onto the precious sheet. My soul cries out, my mind struggles, my hand moves, the pen writes – but how can it inscribe the true nature of that original cry?

June 17.

A day has passed, and only now can I bring myself to write of what occurred when I returned to the glade.

My mind was in a tumult as I made my way through vegetation which steamed in the morning sunlight. Perhaps the distraction of this mental turmoil made my destination seem closer than on my previous visit, for almost before I knew it I was in the glade.

Once again the quiet beauty of the place impressed itself upon me. My busy thoughts subsided, like a millpond when the paddles cease to turn. I raised my face, and allowed the warm light, softened by the foliage overhead, to bathe me. I saw that the glade was within a kind of dome, with the topmost branches of the trees around its perimeter curving gently to meet high above me, their tips brushing together as they swayed in the lightest of breezes.

A sense of great happiness overcame me. I felt as if I had accomplished a difficult but necessary task, and now I could take my ease, and enjoy the fruits of my labour at peace with the world. My surroundings seemed to play an active part in my satisfaction, as though the very spot upon which I stood was allocated especially to me for my delight, and had been awaiting my arrival in order to bring the whole scene to fullness and completion.

My knowledge of myself evaporated like mist. The whispering breeze seemed to blow clear through me, leaving me light and empty. The elusive fragrance I noticed on my first visit was more pervasive than ever. I reached out to touch a vivid blue flower beside me, and found its texture marvellous, like moist velvet. Thoughtlessly I plucked the flower, crushed it gently in my hand, and raised it to my nose. The aroma it released was the fragrance that haunted the entire glade, concentrated into a nectar that thrilled my every nerve. For many moments I basked in the sensations it evoked, quite lost in them.

Then, at the edge of the clearing, I saw it.

The creature was perhaps seven feet tall, standing erect on two legs. It looked like a large ape, but the entire body was covered in fine white hair: the softest fur, so white as to seem radiant. Its lidless eyes were completely round, at least two inches in diameter, and as black as jet, like pools of ink.

The beast remained motionless, seeming to study me. Its gaze was steady and clear, utterly transfixing me. I had the impression of great age, although the creature appeared healthy and robust. Then it raised its hand, palm towards me, in a gesture so human that I gasped. The sensation of shock I received was like a physical blow. However, I was not afraid. Instead, I was filled with a kind of awe. Slowly I raised my own hand, in imitation of the creature's gesture. After a few moments it inclined its head, and I understood it was making a bow to me. I returned the obeisance respectfully. Then the creature turned away from me, stepped among the trees, and vanished from my sight.

I have no recollection of making my way back to my camp, but here I found myself at dusk. As I close this entry tonight I am still unable to comprehend what took place.

June 18.

I have passed the day in my camp, unwilling to stir. Whenever I made an effort to rouse myself a vision of the creature in the glade arose before me, and I could conceive of no task that was not dwarfed by the magnitude of that encounter.

What did I see in the glade? Did it have substance, existing in a world so unfamiliar as to be fantastical, or has my mind become disordered, lending to my imagination that power which it has robbed from my reason? If my faculties have truly become unsound I must resign myself to losing my wits.

Yet, in the midst of confusion, I find a crumb of comfort. Something, at least, has happened. Previously, all my hopes and fears, my speculations and suspicions – all have been insubstantial. But now, undeniably, my life must change. Either I saw that strange being, or I am going mad. I have taken a step into the unknown, and must take another.

June 19.

I was awake at first light, and having no stomach for food I set off immediately. My progress through the forest was marked only by the shrill cries of its inhabitants as they greeted the dawn. I confined my thoughts to the task in hand, and made every effort to prevent my mind from contemplating any other subject, most especially the possible outcome of my journey.

Thus I proceeded until I reached my destination. I paused at the edge of the clearing, gathering my courage, and then I stepped into the little glade.

I confess I was disappointed to find myself alone. Doubts and fears began to assail me. However, no sooner had they arisen than they subsided. Once again, a carefree mood crept over me. My attention was pulled, *gently but firmly, away from the fears and sorrow within me, and was claimed by my surroundings; the play of light and shadow on the bright foliage, the soothing whisper of the rustling treetops, and the exquisite fragrance exuded with limitless generosity by every atom of life in that enchanted place. I threw back my head and drank it in.*

All at once I knew I was watched. I lowered my gaze, expecting, with a tremor of anticipation, to see the creature I encountered on my previous visit. Instead my eyes came to rest upon not one, but three of those incredible beings. They seemed identical in appearance, but I was convinced that the middle of the three was that which had appeared to me when I last stood in that spot. As I recovered from my surprise I marvelled anew at them. Their short, white fur was even more delicate than I remembered, their dark eyes more liquid, and their stature more noble. It occurred to me that I was unable to determine their sex by any outward sign, or by their demeanour.

As I gazed at them, the creature in the centre of the trio opened its mouth, and formed a circular shape with it. From this aperture a low humming sound emerged. It began quietly, but swiftly became louder until its eerie reverberations filled the glade. It was a single note, but somehow it contained within it many harmonies. Then, to my utter astonishment, I began to discern within the deep, vibrating harmonies, the sound of human speech!

I felt my head spin, and for a moment I feared I would fall to the ground. As I struggled to master myself I began to understand that the words I heard were not being spoken by the creature, but arose in my own mind, as though the creature's voice struck a sympathetic chord from some unknown faculty or organ within me, and this organ then produced the utterance of speech. The words which thus formed within my understanding were:

'Do not fear us.'

Until that moment I had, in truth, felt I might be swept away by a swelling wave of terror. But at those words my fear vanished.

Again, the deep, harmonious hum, and this time, 'Do you understand?'

I nodded my head. 'Yes,' I said, in a cracked voice. It was the first word I had uttered aloud in many months.

The creatures nodded their heads, as if in imitation of my action.

'That is well,' I heard. It seemed now that all three spoke to me in one voice. The creatures took several paces towards me, and halted no more than an arm's length away. At once a sensation of great affection filled me, and I longed to embrace them. No sooner had the impulse arisen than I felt their soft fur beneath my fingers, even though I was still two or three feet distant from them.

I began to laugh. I threw back my head and filled the glade with shouts of happiness, which grew louder – until I realised they were not mine alone, and the creatures were sharing my joy. I shook uncontrollably with a mirth beyond the wildest merriment and all the world seemed to join me. I was a child, and the world required nothing of me but innocent play.

The laughter came to an end, having run its natural course, and I was left refreshed and calm.

I heard the words, 'We wish you well.'

I nodded. 'I wish you well also,' I said. Without warning I began to weep. I recalled an incident from my distant childhood. One day, when I was no more than three years old, my mother took me with her to a market town some distance from our home. In the busy throng I became separated from her, and found myself surrounded by unfamiliar faces. I was wracked by fear and misery but manfully I held my tears in check. Well-meaning strangers noticed my plight, and strove to find my mother. At last I saw her face emerging from the crowd. She rushed towards me and swept me up into her arms. The tears which I released at that moment were the same as those which now coursed down my face. Relief, happiness and exhaustion were mingled in them, and as they ceased to flow I saw the trio of creatures appear to confer among themselves.

They turned towards me, and I heard, 'You will see us again.'

I saw they intended to depart, and reached out to them. One put its hand – for it was much more like a hand than an animal's paw – in mine. I was indescribably comforted by its touch, which was warm and delicate. After a few moments the creature indicated, by the slightest pressure, that it wished to withdraw, and I released my hold.

The trio bowed to me, and I imitated their action. Then, each took a swift step backwards, and disappeared. The manner in which they did this was extraordinary. As they stepped back they seemed to lose something of their solidity, as though transformed into painted figures on a flat surface. Then, as they turned away from me, it was like seeing a page in a book being *turned before my eyes until I was presented with an edge, so thin as to be almost imperceptible. For an instant this edge appeared to be a slit, as if a taut sheet of finest silk were stretched before me, and a sharp blade on the other side of it sliced down through it. A light pulsed through this opening and then it was gone, leaving no trace of my three companions.*

I was alone in the tranquillity of the little glade. It was nearly dusk. The treetops were bathed in a crimson tint, while beneath them the myriad blooms and leaves around me presented a tapestry of rich, deep hues. The air was still and limpid, and despite my fatigue I felt a longing to remain in that place. But as the chill of evening began to creep into the glade it restored a sense of reality to me, and I stirred myself to begin my journey back.

Now as I write by the guttering light of a precious candle I am still astounded by the day's events. In my old life I considered myself to be a thoroughly practical man, never prey to superstition, and it pleased me to believe I was one who had no time for nonsense of any kind. But what use is my scepticism to me now? What use my faith, for that matter?

June 20.

Whatever the fate of my soul the requirements of my body remain unchanged. I set out to hunt for food today, obeying a long-standing resolution to maintain at all times a supply of meat that will see me through a week.

I met with moderate success. But as I returned to my camp I was stopped in my tracks by a thought which struck me like a bolt of lightning. It offers an explanation for my recent experiences, and in view of the sceptical nature of my character to which I alluded, I am surprised it did not occur to me before now. My knowledge of medicines is limited, but I know that certain drugs can provoke visions and dreams so vivid that the dreamer believes them to be real. Is it not probable that I have fallen under the influence of such a substance? Only in the glade have I seen those strange creatures, and only there have I apprehended the elusive fragrance I have mentioned. Perhaps there are certain plants in that spot with narcotic effects that are exuded as a scent or vapour. My sight of the otherworldly beings; my feelings of exceptional calmness; the exaltation of my spirits; and my attacks of tears and laughter – all may be caused by the intoxicating influence of these plants. Indeed, I first glimpsed one of those creatures immediately after crushing a flower, raising it to my nose, and deliberately breathing in its scent.

I debated this explanation with myself as I made my way back to my camp, and have continued to do so for many hours. It is entirely plausible, but leaves me dissatisfied. When I was in the glade I felt, for the first time in my life, that I was faced with undeniable evidence of a world beyond our everyday existence. In all the years that I have been a churchgoer and (I trust) a humble Christian worshiper I have never encountered anything I can describe as holiness. I have believed in religious mystery, but I have never felt its presence. By contrast, while the origin and nature of the creatures in the glade may be mysterious, there was no uncertainty about my experience. It was mystery made manifest, and spoke directly to my heart.

But if all this is merely the product of a drugged trance, what then? I am indeed my own worst foe, for now that I can explain the strange events which took place I am more miserable than ever. Another problem remains unsolved: whether I am in the grip of intoxication or madness, what shall I do?

June 21.

What a fool I am. Last night I wrestled with the dilemma

facing me, in an agony of indecision over what course to take. But when I awoke this morning I knew my dilemma to be imaginary, and likewise the notion that I have any choice in the matter. The prospect of passing the long day ahead in a limbo of dreary toil, enlivened only by moments of fear and despair, was intolerable to me.

I knew I was bound to return to the glade. Even if what awaits me there is madness and abandon, the tiresome business of mere survival is just as sure to lead me to insanity.

Thus resolved, I turned my steps towards the glade once more.

As I followed a now-familiar path my thoughts were no less busy than usual, but a part of me seemed divorced from this activity. The surface of my mind was turbulent, but its depths were still.

A glad cry rose to my lips when I stepped into the clearing and saw the three strange beings there, as if awaiting my arrival. I approached them eagerly, and stood before them. They regarded me gravely, and I had an urge to make a gesture of courtesy by speaking first, in demonstration of my gratitude to them.

Unable to think of a more sophisticated conversational gambit, I simply inclined my head and said, 'I have returned.'

I heard the eerie humming sound. 'We are always with you,' they said.

'And when I am not here?'

'You are always here,' they replied.

I sensed a shadow of unease. I sought to frame the question I wished to ask, but whose answer I feared. Again, I found myself incapable of anything but the most simple utterance.

I took a deep breath. 'Are you real?'

The creatures gazed at me wordlessly. Desperation seized me, and I cried, 'Are you products of my mind?'

'Yes,' they replied.

A faintness overcame me, and I fought for breath.

'Be calm,' the creatures told me. 'You see us in your mind, but we are in the world, as you are in the world.'

'I don't understand,' I said.

'You understand. But you cannot explain.'

It was true. However, a part of me stubbornly grasped for elucidation. 'These plants,' I said, touching a nearby bloom, 'do they intoxicate me? Is that why I can see you?'

There was a pause while the creatures considered my question. 'The plants,' they said, 'dispel a darkness that conceals some of the world from you. They help you see. We are not separate from the world.'

As I tried to allow what they said to reveal its meaning, I saw the creatures take a step back. They intended to depart. 'Wait,' I cried, 'don't leave me!'

'We are always with you.'

It was not enough for me. 'I fear to be alone,' I said.

The creatures conferred together. When they turned to me again they seemed to choose their words with careful deliberation. As their gentle humming filled the glade I heard them say, 'Do you wish to remain with us?'

I hesitated, but the answer rose to my lips despite me. 'Yes,' I said.

'If you wish to remain with us,' the voices said, 'you cannot return. And we must change you.'

I struggled to speak. When finally I was able to reply, my voice was a whisper. 'In what way must I be changed?'

'Your thoughts. Your feelings. What you believe yourself to be.'

'Do you mean,' I said, 'that I shall become... a different person?'

There was a pause. Then, softly, 'No. Not a person.'

I trembled. 'What, then?' I cried, 'What shall I become?'

'You will be as we are.'

I made no answer. One of the creatures approached me again, and stood before me. With great tenderness it laid the back of its hand against my belly. An indescribable warmth spread through me, and with it a feeling of great comfort. The creature's large, fathomless eyes were inches from my own. 'We are always with you,' it said.

I was no longer afraid. I heard my own breath, rising and falling deeply and slowly, filling me with peace and stillness.

'You are weary,' the creatures said. 'Go, and rest. Consider what we have said. Return when the sun rises again, and we shall speak.'

The creature took a step back and rejoined its companions. They made me a bow, which I returned, and then they vanished.

June 22.

I have not slept, but as dawn breaks my heart is at rest.

Through the long night I reviewed the events of my life. I saw the bright countenance of every person whom I love, and heard their cheerful voices, and I remembered the peaceful faces of those who have passed from this world. I thought especially of one I love very dearly, and whom I will love always, no matter what becomes of me. I revisited the happy scenes of my childhood, the pleasant haunts of my youth, and every chapter of my manhood, reliving each moment of joy and sorrow.

Finally, I made a reckoning. I will never be rescued from this place. I will never see those faces again, or hear those voices. Meanwhile, every hour is a weary burden to me.

The prospect of changing, of losing all the thoughts and feelings that make me the person I am – or believe myself to be – is full of terror. But how much more terrible is a future in which my precious thoughts do nothing but torment me, and my feelings are only misery, loneliness and despair?

When I began this journal, I imagined the judgment of anyone who might read it. Such a reader will now conclude, beyond doubt, that I have gone mad. 'See,' he will cry, 'the man has abandoned his soul to the darkness.' If he is of a charitable disposition, perhaps he will add, with a shake of his head, 'poor, poor fellow.'

Are you charitable? Whatever judgment you make I will simply tell you, with all my heart, that it is not towards the darkness that I now set out, but the light.

Farewell

*

After I'd read the manuscript and its covering letter for a third time I sat at my desk for an hour or more, and when I finally went to bed I couldn't get to sleep. Eventually I drifted off, and dreamed I was following a dishevelled figure who was trudging towards a jungle he never reached. I woke up briefly at dawn, feeling melancholy. But I went back to sleep, and when I opened my eyes again bright sunlight was glowing behind my curtains.

As soon as I got up I made three decisions. The first was to abandon any attempt to establish the authenticity of what I'd found in the envelope. The previous evening, when I'd been sitting at my desk, it seemed important to know how much – if any – of what I'd read was true. I'd toyed with the idea of trying to identify "George", the author of the covering letter, or his great-uncle Pascoe, or of researching eighteenth century shipwrecks in the hope of finding one to match the castaway who wrote the manuscript that Pascoe discovered. If, that is, Pascoe didn't write it himself, to hoax George, who, in turn, could himself be a hoaxer, and have concocted the whole tale, including a fictitious great-uncle Pascoe. For that matter, "George" himself could be someone's fictional creation.

But even if both George and great-uncle Pascoe were real, and were telling the truth, could I find the "famous" voyage that George says Pascoe undertook? Perhaps the word is being used as a kind of ironic in-joke, in the way that a family will talk about "the famous incident with the duck," or Leonard Cohen refers to the "Famous Blue Raincoat".

Or perhaps everything was true, including the castaway's story.

But I decided it didn't matter.

The second decision was connected to the first, and concerned my personal life. Perhaps I should have mentioned that about four months ago – only eight months after my wife's death – I met a woman I've become very fond of. To be honest it's more than fondness, and I know she reciprocates my feelings.

The last four months have brought me great happiness, but also a shadow of torment. I was married to my late wife for nearly thirty years, and since she died I've been adrift. The new woman in my life represents a kind of landfall – but on an unfamiliar shore, where I remain haunted by the place I left behind. But home, as they say, is where the heart is, and should not be where only memories reside. I have a choice, like the castaway. If I embrace a new life then yes, I will be changed – into a different creature, you could say. But what's the alternative? To roam the wilderness of my grief for the rest of my life, mourning an existence to which I'll never be restored?

The castaway's story helped me decide what to do, and no matter who wrote it, I'm grateful to have read it. My mind is made up. There may be those who'll think I'm mad, or perhaps consider it unseemly for me to remarry so soon. But it's what I'm going to do.

Which brings me to the third decision. I found the manuscript seemingly by chance, and I'd like to pass it on, in the same way that I received it. Perhaps it will bring benefit to a stranger, as it did to me. So, I've put the document back in the envelope and resealed it, having added a page that tells the story of how I found it on a damp day in a grey city.

I considered the possibility of trying to find another junk shop on my travels, and leaving the bible there for someone to discover, or of slipping it into the shelves of a little bookshop somewhere.

But I think the place for a bible is a church. I've never been very religious, although I find I'm becoming more so as I get older. However, my new lover is a churchgoer, even though her interest is as much architectural as doctrinal. She's already told me that if I should ever feel ready to propose to her she will accept, and has indicated where she would like to get married.

I'm very lucky. She's a wonderful, exceptional woman.

One day you may find yourself in a simple early-nineteenth century church with a tranquil, companionable atmosphere, on the outskirts of a mid-sized provincial town. Somewhere in that church – perhaps on a small table, tucked away at the back of the nave behind the rows of neat, plain pews – you may see a bible, about the size of a typical hardback book, with an unadorned cover and a spine bearing traces of gold lettering almost faded away with age.

Be sure to pick it up.

AUTHOR'S NOTE

Thank you for reading these stories, and I hope you enjoyed them. If so, I'd be very grateful if you would let people know. You can give the book a rating on Amazon, which greatly increases the chance of others finding and reading it. As well as a star rating, you'll be asked to enter a review, but it can be just a few words. (If you'd like to write a longer review, I look forward to reading it, but it's not required.)

You can also rate the book on Goodreads, where you can simply give a star rating, or add a review if you'd like to.

If you use Twitter, where I spend far too much time trying to entertain myself and other people, you can follow me there:

@thewritertype

And finally, I have a web site where you can investigate all the other things I do. It has links to my blog and to some podcasts I've made, among other delights:

thewritertype.com

Thank you again, and au revoir.

Printed in Great Britain
by Amazon